ALICE DEVISES AND THE KINGDOM OF LIGHTWOLD

By Jayne Kara

Published by New Generation Publishing in 2013

www.newgeneration-publishing.com

 New Generation Publishing

Chapter One

With the exception of sharing a name with a famous singer, Bill Withers had led an uneventful life. Alcohol had been his addiction and because of it he'd lost his family and everything he owned. Each night he settled into a doorway to shelter from the elements. Each day would be spent in the pursuit of money to buy alcohol or dumpster diving behind Johal's supermarket for food. Legislation means that supermarkets have to discard food items after their display by or use by dates, so the dumpster was a good place to get free, relatively fresh food.

The doorway behind the shop was quite sheltered from the wind and rain, but as Bill ripped open a box of out of date chocolate éclairs, a wind roared down the alleyway forming, what looked to him, like a mini tornado. Black clouds swirled in the sky above the alley and strands of forked lightning flashed and sparked around him. He crouched down and curled into a ball to try to shield himself from the storm but it was over in seconds. The wind, lightning and swirling clouds were gone and standing in front of him was a brown haired, little girl.

For a moment he considered ignoring her and just going about his rummaging, however, behind his degeneracy was a semblance of conscience. The child looked up at him with tearful, big, brown eyes but showed no fear.

"Where's my mummy?" she whispered.

"Er, I dunno," he said and held out his grubby hand to offer her a half eaten chocolate éclair. She timidly took it from him and ate it, smudging chocolate and cream around her mouth. He looked up and down the alleyway. "Where d'you come from kid?" She shook her head. Bill pondered what to do. He knew what he should do, but that would take some effort on his part, and would interfere with his day. But he couldn't just leave the girl standing there. She kept staring at him. "Look, your mum's not down here so why don't you go down the alley and try to find her?" He took her by the shoulder and pointed the way out of the alley. She started to cry. "Alright," he gruffled. "I'll take you." He shuffled out of the doorway and started to walk in the direction of the main road. As they walked she grasped the little finger of his left hand and followed him.

Bill led the little girl into the first shop, a crowded newsagent.

"You know you're not allowed in here Bill," shouted the jobsworth behind the counter. In the past customers had complained about the smell Bill exuded. He'd been asked to leave and not come back.

"Yeah, I found this kid," he said stumbling for words.

"What do you mean you 'found her'?" shrieked an irate female customer. "What are you doing to that little girl?" She pushed Bill out of the way. The other customers gathered around them.

"Has he hurt you love?" someone said. The little girl looked around, bewildered. Bill began to shuffle backwards out of the shop.

"I didn't want any trouble," he mumbled.

"Where d'you think you're going?" someone shouted.

"Someone phone the police!" said a second voice.

"Don't let him get away!" added a third.

"Get him!" yelled the crowd of shoppers.

The little girl was almost trampled in the rumble to apprehend Bill. No one actually wanted to touch him, but they blocked the door so he couldn't get out. Someone hit him on the head with a rolled up newspaper.

"Let me out of here, I just found her, right! I don't want any trouble," Bill yelled. The little girl cried. The customers shouted.

Ten minutes later the police arrived in two different blue, yellow and white cars, to try to sort out the situation, and to take Bill and the little girl away. As the police helped Bill into the back seat of one of the police cars, he regretted ever trying to help the girl. A police woman found a name on the label of the girl's red coat – Alice Devises.

"That's got to be her name!"

"Is your name Alice honey?"

The little girl nodded.

"You're a little beauty aren't you? Where's your mum and dad sweetheart?"

The girl shrugged, her eyes filled with tears.

Once at the police station Bill was taken to an interrogation room containing simply a table with a couple of chairs and recording equipment. A doctor was sent for, to examine the little girl. Alice caused quite a stir in the police station. The officers and support staff all gathered around her giving her chocolate and sweets.

Over the next three hours Bill told his story again and again to one policeman after another, about how he'd been rummaging for food in the bins behind Johal's supermarket and the girl had appeared in a tornado and flash of lightning. They gave him tea and biscuits.

"What do you think?" new recruit PC Ainsworth said to his older colleague, Sergeant Digby, as they left the interrogation room. "Do you reckon he's telling the truth?"

"Bill's a waster but I don't think he's a kidnapper or that he would ever hurt a kid. I've been arresting him for years to get him out of doorways and on drunk and disorderly charges, but nothing more serious than that. The thunder and lightning story's a bit far fetched. That's probably the booze talking. Have there been any reports about missing kids?" Sergeant Digby asked the red haired WPC who sat at the reception desk.

"No Sir!" she replied. "It's weird isn't it? Surely someone should be missing a kid of that age."

"Call Social Services. We'll let them deal with her for now. You'd better let Bill go – we know where to find him if we need to talk to him again."

Chapter Two

Seven Years Later

Alice lay on her back, her feet on the wall, in her bedroom, staring at a poster of a tousled haired Justin Beiber on the ceiling. It was a nice room, painted girly pink, and she felt comfortable here, her eighth foster placement in seven years, but she knew she'd blown it. That car didn't set itself on fire! She felt nervous – that's the trouble with care – nothing is permanent – you never know where you're going to be placed or with whom.

Alice was Betty and Barry Briggs' first foster kid and she was not what they'd wanted. They'd wanted a baby – or at least someone under five – not a pre-pubescent arsonist who'd had almost as many foster homes as birthdays. Not that she'd ever had real birthdays.

She never meant to start fires – they just kind of happened. The first one started at school when she'd been ordered to tidy a store cupboard. It had been full of dusty junk which Alice thought would look better on a bonfire. Next thing she knew there was smoke and flames and she was escaping for her life. There were alarm bells ringing and people screaming, the school kids being evacuated and fire engines and the police asking her questions for hours on end. Then there was the car....

This was a nice placement. The house had its own drive and the street was lined with trees. Betty and Barry, a middle aged couple with no kids, were nice people – simple and a bit square – but kind. Betty knitted toys for the poor and Barry played golf. Alice really hadn't meant to blow it.

Downstairs she heard Betty crying and Barry's one sided conversation as he shouted down the telephone.

"Yes! A fire! The car! On the drive! No! There's no-one else it could have been! No – no-one was hurt. Yes, yes, you have to come and get her. We can't look after her any more. What if she sets fire to the house? She's too dangerous!"

Alice stood up and pulled her small pale blue suitcase down from the top of the wardrobe to pack her few belongings. She'd done this so many times before it was becoming almost routine. T shirts, skirts, jeans, spare trainers – no photos, nothing precious. Some foster kids didn't even have suitcases for their stuff and had to use black bin bags when they were moved on. That's the life of a foster kid! Alice put the mobile phone Betty had bought for her in her pocket and packed the charger in her suitcase. She wasn't going to give the phone back.

The door bell rang and there was a mumble of voices.

"Alice! Are you packed?" Barry yelled angrily.

"Coming!" she replied. She took one last look around her pretty bedroom and wished she could reach the Justin Beiber poster to take with her, but she couldn't really ask Barry to get it down. Not after destroying his car. At that moment the poster fell from the ceiling and floated to the floor.

"Cool!" she shrugged, and rolled it up.

With the poster rolled under her arm, she dragged her suitcase across the landing and down the staircase. Before her stood a tall man, dressed all in black, whom she'd never seen before. He was unshaven and wore a black wide brimmed hat. Alice thought he looked like a cowboy.

"Alice," he said with a huge smile. He had a gold

tooth that flashed when he smiled.

"Who are you? You're not my usual social worker. Where's Ellie?"

"You can call me Herb. Ellie is away on holiday and as this is an emergency I've been asked to collect you."

"Fine. You done all the paperwork?" she asked, demonstrating knowledge of procedure unusual for her age. He smiled again.

"Everything is in order," he replied.

"That was quick. It usually takes weeks."

Betty and Barry shuffled awkwardly in the hallway.

"See ya!" Alice said as she picked up her bag and made for the front door. Betty moved forward to hug her. Alice took the hug stiffly and did not reciprocate.

"Bye darling! I'm sorry it didn't work out. If you've forgotten anything we'll send it on to you," Betty said with genuine tears in her eyes. Alice stared at Betty and felt annoyed.

What do they know? They'll never know what it's like to be passed around from place to place – never having a real home, she thought, but she kept quiet. What was the point in complaining? Nothing ever changed.

"Yeah sure! Come on Herb! Let's get on to the next place," she said as she pushed passed the adults.

**

As they sat in Herb's blue Fiat Punto Alice looked back sadly at her eighth foster placement and the burnt out car on the drive. She really had no idea how that fire had started. One moment she'd been waiting to go shopping with Betty. She'd been thinking about how hot and stuffy it was in the car, when the silent engine had started smoking. Seconds later there were flames. Luckily for Alice the car did not have child locks and

9

she'd managed to escape out of the back doors.

Outside the Briggs' house, Herb started his car and he and Alice drove away.

Two hours later social worker Ellie Jones arrived at the Briggs' home to collect Alice.

Chapter Three

"So where we going then?" Alice asked. "I've been through a load of foster homes in Warwickshire – there can't be many left. Am I going residential? I hate them places. You have to share your room with people you don't like."

"No, you're going to a boarding school!" Herb answered.

"A WHAT! They're like Borstals! I ain't that bad – there's got to be somewhere else. I told everybody I didn't mean to burn their bloody car!"

"Calm down Alice, this place is different."

"Oh yeah I bet it is. It'll be a prison with bars on the windows and worse still they'll make me wear a uniform! I tell you Herb. I'll escape!"

"Alice – listen to me! There are things you don't know and it's my job to explain them to you."

"There's a McDonalds," she said. Her stomach was churning with nerves and she wanted to stave off the inevitable horror of settling in to a new placement. "I'm starving. Can we go and get something to eat? I want a thick shake." She was used to getting her own way with social workers. They were a push over.

Herb pulled into McDonalds' car park and parked the car. Once inside the restaurant Alice chose a Big Mac meal and strawberry thick shake. Herb had a cup of scalding hot McDonalds' tea. He chose a table in a fairly secluded corner.

"Alice, do you remember your parents?" he asked as she tucked into her Big Mac. She shook her head.

"No I was really young when they dumped me!" she replied.

"They didn't dump you Alice. They sent you here to save your life!"

Herb paused. She looked at him suspiciously.

"Are you kidding me? No one knows what happened to my parents or who I really am, or where I came from. That screwed me in the system. I had no identity – no birth certificate – that meant I couldn't get adopted when I was little, and then later, no one wants an older kid who miraculously starts fires by accident. But you know all this – you ARE the system!"

"No Alice, I am not a social worker," Herb replied.

"You what! Oh my God I've been kidnapped!" she exclaimed. She looked around and prepared to scream for help but as she did, she noticed all the staff and customers appeared to be frozen. Fries that a child had knocked off a table were hanging in the air. A woman was mid sneeze. Everything was silent.

"What the Hell!"

"I'm not going to hurt you," said Herb. "I just need you to listen to me. That is one of my powers Alice. I can freeze time in the immediate area. It is very useful if you ever need to escape from a – let's say - tricky situation."

"What! How?"

"I am a warlock. My name is Lighthorne Herb. I have been sent from Lightwold on the island of Hy Brasil which is off the west coast of Ireland, to bring you back." There was something about Herb's voice that was hypnotic and calming.

"Holy crap! You actually believe what you're saying, don't you?" Alice said. "You're a freaking nutcase!"

"Stop using profanities Alice," he said sternly. "Have you never wondered why fires start around you or why, whenever you wish for something, it happens?"

"I've been wishing for parents and a home all my life but that's never happened," she replied stubbornly.

"Simple things Alice."

"So am I a warlock then?"

"No you are part genie, part warlock or witch. That makes you a very powerful being."

"Get out! You mean like – I grant you three wishes – I get stuck in a bottle – like genie!"

"Sort of. A lot of the mythology has been skewed over time."

"I don't want to get stuck in a bottle."

"You won't get stuck in a bottle."

"Part witch? Can I fly around on broomsticks like they do in fairy stories?"

"Maybe, at some point. You are also descended from the witches of Pendle, on your father's side of the family. But Alice, I need to get you to the training school Bonneville Goodhouse in Lightwold. The autumn term begins in two days time."

"This is crazy! Are you sure you ain't a pervert?" she asked. Herb shook his head. She continued, "But it kind of makes sense. All the weird things that have happened in my life. Like the time when Jack, one of my foster brothers was picking on me, I wished something bad would happen to him and a shelf fell down and bonked him on the head. And when Milly Pruett was bullying me at school, calling me white trash, the next day she got measles," she gabbled. All her life she'd been praying something wonderful would happen. It was unbelievable and she was scared but she wanted to believe what Herb was saying. "So what's this Lightwold then?"

Herb smiled but said sternly:

"You will be attending the Bonneville Goodhouse training academy for magical creatures in Lightwold on the island of Hy Brasil, and yes – you will have to wear a uniform. There you will learn to control your powers. You cannot hurt humans with them. It's wrong."

"Jack and Milly deserved it," Alice said with a grin

13

and took a deep slurp of her thick shake. Herb sighed. "So now I have to change schools again. Well, it's not so bad doing it at the beginning of term. Like, it's horrible being the new kid half way through a term when everybody already knows each other. And what d'you mean – humans? We're all humans ain't we?"

"Not exactly," he replied. "It's a really long story but the abridged version is that you are an Ethereal. You're one of the numerous magical species that came to this world many years ago." Alice looked at him dubiously.

"How many years?" she asked.

"I don't know exactly how many years ago, perhaps tens of thousands, perhaps more."

"So we're aliens?"

"Not exactly. We are more inter-dimensional than extra-terrestrial beings."

"Well you're not explaining this very well. I don't know what the Hell that means. I think you're just some whack job pervert making up some weird creepy story to trick me. Then they'll find my body in a ditch! I can see the headlines – KID NOBODY WANTED – MURDERED!"

"If this isn't true, how have I frozen all these people?" he asked, becoming frustrated. She shrugged and tried to think of an explanation.

"If you were really magic you'd be able to cool that tea down enough to drink," Alice said with a smile. Herb tapped the cardboard cup with his index finger then picked up the tea and drank it in one gulp.

"Does that prove my point?" he asked her.

"That is pretty impressive," she acknowledged. "McDonalds' tea is really hot and their apple pies are even hotter. Can I have an apple pie?"

"No! You've had enough for now and I don't want to queue up again," said Herb. Alice pouted as Herb continued. "We are not exactly immortal, but we do live a very long time. We can however die in accidents or in battle."

"How long do these Ethereals live then?"

"That's not relevant."

"How old are you?"

"One hundred and fifty nine," he replied.

"Yeah right! Now I know you're lying! I mean you look really old – like thirty or something – but you ain't a hundred and something. I saw a giant tortoise once that was like – ancient, and he had a really scraggly neck. You ain't got a scraggly neck. Did you know my parents?" she asked. He nodded. "Tell me about them then"

"Zephyr – who mythology says, was one of the Greek gods. He was in love with your beautiful mother Chloris," he began.

"She was a genie, right?" Alice asked.

"Yes, but she was in love with your father. The warlock, Sion.

Such a confluence of powers is unusual. In fact no one ever realised warlocks and genies, or to use the correct term – djinn – could ever have children together. Zephyr was not only jealous of the love they had for each other but also of the power their progeny would hold."

"What's progeny?"

"You are their progeny. You have the powers of both genie and warlock. Zephyr wanted your power so, in short, he tried to kidnap you. There was a battle during which, your mother sent you to the human world. Your parents were killed in the battle."

"Is a warlock a wizard?"

"No – we don't need wands or anything like that."

"When's my birthday?" Herb sighed again and shook his head.

"New Years Day."

"Cool! This Zephyr – you say he was a Greek god," Herb nodded. "So gods are real?" Herb nodded again. "So what about the god everyone prays to?"

"You mean the God of Christianity, Islam and Judaism?" he asked. This time it was Alice's turn to nod. "Just because there is an order of very powerful creatures, does not mean there isn't a being even more powerful than all of them, and who in fact created them. Some Ethereals call themselves 'Gods' because ignorant, uneducated humans in the past used to bow down and worship them. In truth, none of them ever created anything as wonderful as the earth and they did not create you or me," Herb said seriously. Alice was confused, what he was saying was overwhelming, but decided not to press his answer.

"There is one more thing. It is possible," he said seriously, "that at some point in the future, Zephyr may come back and try again to kidnap you or steal your powers." Alice's eyes widened. She looked terrified. "Don't worry! Protective measures have been put in place and there is no way he can get into the school. You will be far safer at the school than out in the human world."

"How can you be sure?" Alice asked fearfully, she didn't like what she was hearing.

"Everyone at the school has your best interests at heart. You will be safe," he assured her. "We have to leave now Alice." He rose from his seat. "What are you doing?" he asked as she took out her mobile phone.

"I'm checking the internet for Hy Brasil," she replied. "McDonalds have got free wi-fi."

"Put it away Alice, we have to get going."

"How are we going to get there? Can we fly?" Alice asked.

"We don't fly in front of mortals," he replied as he

waved his hand and the restaurant returned to normal.

"I meant on a plane!"

Chapter Four

As Herb and Alice drove along the winding A5 road through north Wales, thick, black clouds swirled over head. Sheet lightning flashed across the sky making it look as if there was a strobe light behind the clouds. Four hours and two stops later they reached Holyhead to board a car ferry, to cross the Irish Sea to Dublin. Alice talked the whole way.

"I've never been on a ferry," she announced as they left the car in the hold of the ship to go up on deck. "I've only seen the sea twice. Once I spent a wet week in a caravan with, I think, my fourth foster carers, and when I was in residential care they took all the kids to Skegness for a wet weekend. It was cool! I like the sea."

Alice was getting tired, but was too excited to calm down. Even though it was mid summer the sea was grey and large waves crashed across the bow of the boat. She ran to the deck rail to watch the sea and the sky but Herb pulled her away.

"What's wrong? Why can't I stand by the edge?"

"It's dangerous!"

"But you're magic! You could stop time and save me," she squealed.

"We don't use magic like that!" he replied becoming exasperated. "And I don't think even I could freeze the sea." He wasn't used to dealing with children. Herb took hold of Alice's arm and led her into the ferry's cafeteria. Alice helped herself to some leaflets advertising attractions in Dublin and Eire, and made Herb stand in line for food and drinks. Once they had been served, they sat down at a table with orange plastic chairs that were fixed to the structure of the boat.

"Why couldn't you freeze the sea? What's the

biggest thing you can freeze? Why can't we use magic all the time? I can't wait to use magic. It's gonna be great," she said whilst biting into a cheese and onion sandwich.

"Oh my God Herb – look! I'm famous," Alice squealed, pointing to a television which was attached to the wall above the cash register and cashier. On the screen, to the left of the newsreader, an old school photo of Alice was prominently displayed. A red banner rolled right to left across the bottom of the picture. It read: BREAKING NEWS – 11 YEAR OLD ALICE DEVISES FROM WARWICKSHIRE HAS BEEN KIDNAPPED FROM HER FOSTER PLACEMENT BY A MAN POSING AS A SOCIAL WORKER. There were pictures of a distraught Betty and Barry being interviewed by news reporters.

"I'm on TV! What are we going to do Herb?"

Herb looked around. No one was paying any attention to the television. Everyone was too involved in their own meals, conversations with their travelling companions or playing with their mobile phones. It appeared people were oblivious to what was going on around them.

"We're alright Alice – no one has noticed," Herb said.

"That's the story of my life – no one ever notices me – until I start a fire or something." The news story changed and Alice relaxed.

"How far is it now? How long is it going to take? What is Lightwold? How many other kids there? Are we nearly there yet?" Alice's list of questions was endless.

Herb answered most of her questions with, "Wait and see," which she found infuriating.

"Are you a teacher at this school?"

"No, I'm more of an administrator," he replied.

"What does that mean?"

"I deal with the running of the school. Making sure there are enough food supplies and that all the classrooms are equipped."

The ferry docked in Dublin. Alice and Herb returned to the hold of the ship and climbed back into the blue car. Herb drove off the ferry and exited the docks.

"We're in Dublin – right?" she asked. Herb nodded. "Good! I want to go to the zoo. Look," she waved one of the advertising leaflets in front of his face. "There's a zoo in Dublin and I want to go."

"No, we don't have time," he replied firmly.

"That's not fair!" she whined and folded her arms across her chest. "I'm really bored."

"Besides," he continued. "It's nearly five o'clock. The zoo will be closing soon." She checked the leaflet.

"Damn it!" she swore under her breath. Herb was right. The zoo was already closed for the day. He headed the car westwards again. They passed through the city of Dublin and several smaller towns. It was all unfamiliar to Alice. They travelled onwards, along the M4 and N6 toll roads, across Eire through miles of countryside. Herb had hoped to complete his retrieval mission in a single day, but with so many food and toilet stops the journey was taking far longer than he'd planned.

"Why is everything so green?" Alice asked Herb, pressing her nose against the window, as mile after mile passed. "I'm bored. There's nothing to look at. Where are all the people?"

"It's called the countryside and this part of Eire is fairly sparsely populated," he replied. "Don't you think it's beautiful?"

"I think it's green and there are a lot of cows, but I can't get a signal on my phone any more," Alice answered petulantly. "Countryside is boring."

As night fell, Alice finally dropped off to sleep in the car, and Herb pulled into the car park of a small hotel. He parked the car and booked separate rooms for Alice and himself, then carried her in from the car. He laid her on top of her bed then went to his own adjoining room.

Alice slept soundly. Herb wanted to be sure Alice was safe from the dangers he knew she faced. He also wanted to ensure she wouldn't try running away if she woke in the night, so he spent the hours of darkness in an arm chair dozing sporadically.

When she awoke in the morning Alice changed her clothes, washed and met up with Herb downstairs and they ate a buffet breakfast together. The hotel staff eyed the miss matched pair suspiciously but if they'd seen the news reports, they said nothing. When she thought no one was looking she hid some croissants and iced buns in her pocket. After Alice and Herb had eaten, they set off travelling westwards once more. The car smelled musty and Alice was a little quieter now. She spent the journey time playing games on her phone. They reached County Mayo and, after a brief stop for lunch, headed for the Michael Davitt swing bridge to cross to Achill Island. Finally Alice had something interesting to look at!

Alice was quite impressed with the bridge. Its metallic supports looked to her as if they were driving through a giant's bony ribcage. Herb and Alice had to wait as the bridge opened to let three small fishing boats pass through. The sailors on the boats waved to Alice as they sailed by. The air smelled fishy.

"That bloke looks like the sea captain out of the Simpsons," Alice yelled to Herb as she excitedly waved back.

"I don't know who the Simpsons are," Herb replied seriously.

"Never mind," she sighed. *He must be really stupid,* she thought, and then added sarcastically: "They probably don't live around here."

Once the bridge had closed, they drove on to Achill Island, and finally down narrow roads to the small village of Dooega. Most of the houses in the village were single storey, painted white and randomly dotted across a hillside facing the sea, not set in lines as they are in most towns and villages. The landscape was strange and unfamiliar, and the air was fresh and smelled of the ocean. The village was set in a bay surrounded by rocky outcrops.

"Bring your suitcase Alice," Herb said as he stopped the car outside a tiny isolated cottage which was almost covered in pink rambling roses and, looked like the picture on top of a chocolate box Alice had received as a present last Christmas.

"Can't you carry my case? It's heavy. Are we at Lightwold? This place isn't very big. What are we doing here?" Alice asked.

"Just wait and see!" Herb snapped and didn't take her case from her. He knocked, three sharp raps, on the small, arched, wooden front door. The door was opened by a tall woman with long grey hair which floated over her shoulders. She wore a floor length grey silk dress, with long trailing sleeves, and Alice noted that everything about the woman was long, thin and grey. She wasn't old, but she wasn't exactly young either.

"Alice!" she announced warmly. "Welcome! Come in! Come in!" The door opened straight into a small, over filled, single living room.

"I need to use your loo! I'm busting!" Alice said frantically bobbing from one leg to another. Herb sighed again.

"If you didn't drink so many fizzy drinks all the time you wouldn't need the bathroom so often."

"I'm a kid – it's what we do!"

"The bathroom is through the kitchen," the tall woman said, pointing towards the rear of the house.

"It's not an outside loo is it?" Alice asked with concern as she hopped from one foot to the other.

"No, we do have indoor plumbing Alice," the woman replied. Alice pushed passed her and quickly made her way to the bathroom. "You look tired Herb."

"You can't imagine how irritating and tiring children are!" he replied angrily. "Questions! Questions! Questions! She never stops talking – who – what – when – why - it's so mind numbingly annoying. I've never met such a hyperactive eleven year old. And she never stops eating."

When Alice returned from the bathroom, Herb and the woman were sitting in the tiny living room. The room was full of sparkling ornaments, candles and knick knacks and Alice thought Herb and the woman both looked much too big for such a small space.

"Alice, this is Rosebay Thistledown," Herb said.

"So we're not at Bonneville Goodbody or whatever it's called yet?" Alice sighed.

"Bonneville Goodhouse," Herb corrected.

"Whatever! We're still not there! Herb we've been travelling for days," she whined petulantly.

"Alice you're being rude! Say hello to Rosebay."

"Yeah hi! But I'm hungry and tired and I'm fed up of travelling. And you wouldn't take me to the zoo. How much further is it? And have you got wi-fi?" she asked Rosebay.

"No I'm sorry I don't, but I can see you're eager to get on. It's not much further Alice," Rosebay answered. "You can use my row boat to get to your final means of travel."

"What does that mean?"

"Wait and see," Rosebay said with a grin. Alice

sighed with frustration.

Rosebay snapped her fingers and a selection of cakes, pastries and sandwiches appeared on plates on a coffee table in front of Alice. She sat down and tucked into the food, ravenously.

"These are cool!" Alice said. "I'm starving. What are you then? Genie or witch?"

"I'm an elf," Rosebay replied.

"I thought elves were short and wore green hats," said Alice with a mouthful of pastries.

"No, we are quite different from the Christmas card effigies you often see," Rosebay answered softly. "More guardians of nature than wrappers of Christmas presents."

Rosebay and Herb watched Alice devouring the food. She finished everything on the table and wiped her mouth with a tissue. Rosebay snapped her fingers and the empty plates disappeared.

"That beats washing up. Got any coke?"

A glass of coke appeared in front of her.

"It is time to undertake the final leg of your journey Alice," Rosebay told her. "You can leave your luggage here. I'll have it transported to the school as soon as possible."

Alice sipped her drink. When she was ready, Herb, Rosebay and Alice left the cottage to walk to Trá Mór Strand; a three kilometre long sandy beach on Achill Island's south facing Atlantic shore. The wind whipped around them blowing sand into Alice's face.

"I hate the beach," Herb said, looking sympathetically at Alice.

"It's only sand," she replied. "I like the seaside no matter how windy it is. It's better than being in a town." They continued walking in silence. It occurred to Alice that she'd put her trust and safety into the hands of complete strangers but in a weird way it all seemed right. As yet, they hadn't hurt her and it had already been quite an adventure – so far. Rosebay led them to a short, rickety, wooden pier with a small yellow row boat moored at the end.

Chapter Five

Alice, Herb and Rosebay walked to the end of the wooden pier and all stood, side by side, looking out to sea. Alice's stomach was doing summersaults with excitement. The sun was hovering above the horizon and as it did the sky glowed tangerine and scarlet. The clouds floated like fluffy pink marshmallows. A pod of giant, grey fin whales broke the surface just off shore, next to a buoy which was bobbing up and down in the water.

"Whoa! Look!" Alice exclaimed.

"Come, we have to row out to them," said Herb.

"This is crazy – they'll kill us! They are monsters! Their tails alone are bigger than me," Alice squealed as she shuffled backwards. "I'm not going out there. I can only swim a little bit. I don't want to drown."

"You'll be perfectly safe Alice," Herb said reassuringly.

"No I don't want to! I'm scared they'll eat me."

"Nothing will eat you Alice," said Rosebay calmly.

"More's the pity," Herb whispered angrily under his breath. Herb leapt into the little yellow row boat and helped Alice and Rosebay to step down.

"Don't be scared Alice. The whales are our friends. They have taken us to Lightwold this way for all time. And we protect them from anyone who would want to hurt them," Rosebay said as she glared at Herb.

The whales waited patiently in the deep water. Positioned on the back of the first whale was a glass howdah, a four sided carriage usually seen on the backs of elephants, ready to transport Alice and Herb to the island of Hy Brasil.

Alice clung nervously to Rosebay's arm as they sat next to each other in the row boat whilst Herb took the oars. Rosebay stared silently watching the sun. Within a few minutes they were next to the whales. It looked to Alice as if they were smiling.

"That one is definitely going to eat us," she insisted – pointing to the first whale in the pod. "Look they're all grinning at us. It's creepy!" The boat bobbed up and down next to the first of the gigantic creatures.

"Don't be rude Alice. Good day Beibhinn," Herb said, addressing the whale as he urged Alice to climb an unnecessarily elaborate red and gold rope ladder which led up the side of the whale into the howdah. Beibhinn snorted a flume of water from her blow hole. Rosebay remained in the row boat.

"Aren't you coming with us?" Alice called to Rosebay.

"Someone has to take the row boat back. Don't worry Alice I'll see you very soon."

They bade farewell to Rosebay and once they were safely inside the howdah, Herb closed the glass door. Beibhinn moved gently forward, gliding across the surface of the ocean. There were eight dark red velvet seats in the howdah. Five faced forwards and three faced back. Herb and Alice took two forward facing seats. The sea was remarkably calm but Alice grasped her seat tightly as she watched Rosebay rowing back to the wooden pier.

"Oh my God! Sharks! They could attack Rosebay!" Alice screamed as she saw three ominous black fins circling Biebhinn. Herb smiled.

"They're dolphins not sharks," Herb replied. "They are as friendly as the whales. There are blue sharks and basking sharks in the water, but none that would hurt you." Alice did not look convinced. The dolphins leapt joyfully in and out of the water.

"How long will it take now? Will it be dark when we get there Herb?" she asked nervously.

"No, at this time of year the days are long and the sun takes a long time to set. We have another hour of daylight at least."

"How is it, the island isn't seen by planes and ships and things?" Alice asked.

"Hy Brasil can't be approached by any normal methods," Herb continued. "It is shielded by magic rendering the island invisible to satellites and disappears when humans approach whether by sea or by air. It's like it exists in a parallel dimension. Only creatures of magical descent can see through the veil. Occasionally on clear days the island has been spotted by sensitive humans from the west coast of the Irish mainland. It vanishes after seconds into the swell of the Atlantic Ocean, and it has been the foundation of many great, ancient Irish folklore tales.

Hy Brasil is protected by ancient spells to make it inaccessible to the outside world. Lost sailors have sometimes glimpsed the island only to have it disappear as they approach. Since the human inventions of planes and satellites, extra spells have had to be invoked to make the island invisible from above."

"Does everyone travel by whales to the island?"

"No there are other ways on and off Hy Brasil. We can sail or fly or teleport, but I wanted you to experience the wonder of whale travel."

"It is pretty wonderful," Alice agreed as she gazed in awe at Beibhinn, the whale, surf across the top of the waves. Alice grew slightly more confident and moved to the front of the howdah to watch as they sailed gracefully across the ocean. The journey took less than twenty minutes and as they approached the island of Hy Brasil, Alice saw a small village with a dock which looked similar to the town of Dooega that they had just left. Beibhinn glided to the end of a large pier that was jutting out into the sea.

"Is the sea here deep enough for the whales?" Alice asked with concern.

"Yes it is very deep. You must never play on the pier or the dock," Herb replied. "Only the Mer people are safe here."

"I'll try to remember that. Did you say Mer people? What, like mermaids?"

"No – not like the human idea of mermaids. The people who live on the dock are more comfortable in the water than we would be, but they don't have fish tails. They are good swimmers and do, however, have gills in their necks.

What you have to remember, you are not human and, you will have to forget the human perception and fairy stories you have been taught."

As they alighted from the howdah Herb thanked Beibhinn, and several dock workers came forward to remove the howdah from her back.

"Is this Lightwold?" Alice asked.

"Yes – this is the town of Lightwold. It's only a few more miles to Bonneville Goodhouse."

"Miles! Oh God we don't have to walk do we? Can't you at least use some magic now and zap us there?"

"Alice Devises – I do believe you are an extremely lazy child!"

"But we've been travelling for DAYS Herb!" she moaned. "I can't go on any longer." Herb laughed as a vehicle, similar to a golf buggy, pulled up beside them, driven by one of the Mer people. Alice stared rudely when she saw the gills in the mer man's neck ripple as he breathed

"Your wish is my command your ladyship," Herb said sarcastically. "We have transport."

Twenty minutes later they passed through a pair of tall iron gates. Across the gates, on a plaque, were the words *BONNEVILLE GOODHOUSE TRAINING ACADEMY* and in smaller letters – *ENTER AT YOUR OWN PERIL.*

Chapter Six

Through the gates, ahead of Alice, was a vista of glorious elm trees interspersed with copper beach trees, each as tall as sky scrapers lining the road leading to Bonneville Goodhouse training school. One tree blocked the road, but, its trunk was fifteen feet in diameter and a tunnel had been cut through it, wide enough for two buggies to pass through simultaneously. On either side of the road were rolling fields which stretched to the horizon. Sheep and the occasional oak tree were dotted around the field. In the distance were lavender, snow-capped mountains which reached to the horizon. The Montes Lunae or Mountains of the Moon range cut the island of Hy Brasil almost in half from northeast to southwest. Narrow passes ran though the mountains connecting Lightwold and Dhuridhin on the other side of the island. The Immortal Forest ran in a semi-circle around the rear of the school building.

On the front lawn in front of the school was a row of five monoliths similar to the Easter Island heads. Alice had seen pictures of the heads in books and on the internet. They were rising in order from the ground, like a wave, then, again in order, sinking back into the ground.

"Uhh," said the first as it reached its zenith.

"Ba," said the second.

"Guh," said the third.

"Ba," said the fourth.

"Ba," said the fifth.

"Why are they making that noise?" Alice asked.

"That's their names," Herb replied impatiently.

"What, do you mean three of them are called 'Ba'?"

"Why not? You're not the only Alice in the world. It's just coincidence three of them happen to be called

'Ba'."

"Where do they come from?"

"I've no idea Alice," he sighed. "They've been here since the beginning of Hy Brasil. Many thousands of years." In truth, Herb knew a great deal about the history of the giant heads, that they had been transported from the magical island of Zelda in the South Pacific Ocean, but he was tired and wanted his retrieval mission over, and couldn't be bothered to explain anything else to Alice.

**

Bonneville Goodhouse School was built with bisque coloured Bath stone, square in shape and each side faced one of the compass points. It had castle like turrets in each corner. The external walls were decorated with strips or bands of curling marble carved into elaborate shapes. There were grotesques, arabesque and candelabra alcoves filled with fantastical creatures, garlands of flowers and scenes from mythology - designs typical of a Gothic style of architecture.

There were five floors. The basement held the kitchens and the maintenance staff living quarters. On the ground floor were reception rooms and offices plus several training rooms. On the first floor were more training rooms and faculty quarters were on the second. The students were divided into house groups, North, South, East and West and lived in studies which were located on the third floor. The attic rooms at the top of the building were for storage. Behind the school was a gymnasium and sports centre, tennis courts and sports fields

Bonneville Goodhouse was a magical building with many towers and turrets, built over a thousand years ago by a myriad of magical beings to protect the children of the supernatural and ensure their education and development. The school backed on to a huge, almost impenetrable forested area called the Immortal Forest. Beyond the forest was a canyon, the size of Cheddar Gorge, and to the north was Bottomless Lake. The lake water was black and no one had ever dived to the bottom – hence the name.

Alice had never seen a building so huge or magnificent. The tree-lined road led to the west face of the building. They stepped out of the buggy and climbed the marble stairs which led to a grand entrance. Great oak doors, elaborately carved, stood four metres tall and the main door knob was above Alice's head, but there was a normal size door inserted into the large doors.

Herb pulled on a silver handle to the right of the smaller front door. It rang the door bell which boomed and sounded as if it was echoing around the whole school, like a great church bell.

The small door within a door creaked open and a tiny, grey haired old lady, little taller than Alice, stood before her.

"Alice Devises!" the woman announced loudly. "You're finally here! Welcome home child. I am Athena Goddessbloom. I am headmistress and founder of Bonneville Goodhouse! I am sometimes known as Aeval – an Irish fairy queen. I have been known by many names over the past few thousands of years."

Alice stepped through the door into a vast hallway. She gazed around in awe. The reception hallway had a black and white chequered floor and sweeping oak staircases. The walls were lined with sumptuous mirrors and antique paintings of former students/teachers, and weird and wonderful creatures. At the top of the staircase were twenty portraits of the former kings of Lightwold, all named Atlas and numbered I to XX. A gargantuan chandelier, dripping with glass diamonds, hung from the centre of the ceiling shining with the light of countless candles.

"Wow! This is really big," Alice said to Herb. "So where can I get something to eat? I'm starving."

"This way Miss Devises," said Miss Goddessbloom.

"Do you meet everybody at the front door? Surely you've got someone to do that for you?"

"No Miss Devises I do not usually open the front door, but we have been waiting for you for a long time, and I just happened to be passing when you rang the doorbell," the head teacher replied.

"So what are you – like a dwarf or something?" Alice asked.

"ALICE!" Herb exclaimed.

"Miss Devises has no-one ever taught you manners?" Miss Goddessbloom said indignantly.

"They tried but it didn't work," Alice replied cheekily. "Why? Have I said something I shouldn't?"

"I was once the Greek goddess Athena," Miss Goddessbloom announced proudly, suddenly appearing much taller than before. "Worshipped by millions. Perhaps the most beautiful woman in the world. We all get old Miss Devises. Five thousand years takes its toll."

"Well you look good for it!" Alice lied with an impish smile.

Herb and Miss Goddessbloom both sighed with exasperation.

"Let's get you settled in your room, and then you can come down for supper. Miss Thorne," she called to a maid who was hovering in the background, "take Miss Devises to West Wing room 17."

The maid stepped forward. She was a small, thin girl with mousey brown hair, who looked about seventeen years old but could have been younger. She was dressed all in black with the exception of a little white apron around her waist and a white bonnet on her head.

"Hello, I'm Alice," Alice said to the girl.

"She doesn't need to know that," Miss Goddessbloom snapped. "And Miss Thorne, please make sure next time the doorbell rings, you are available to answer it!"

"Yes Miss," the girl replied sheepishly and gave a little curtsey.

"Alice," said Herb. "I'll let you get settled in and I'll probably see you later at supper or tomorrow." Alice looked at Herb anxiously. "Don't worry you're perfectly safe. Go with Miss Thorne, I need to talk with Miss Goddessbloom."

"Come on Miss," said the maid, "let me show you your room." Alice followed the girl up the staircase which lined the left hand wall of the hallway.

"Why was Miss Goddessbloom so mean to you?" Alice asked as soon as they were out of earshot.

"Oh, because I'm no one Miss," the girl replied. "Not special like you magical folks."

"You're human then?"

"No Miss," the girl giggled. "Me and my folks - we're the skitters! We clean up and fetch and carry, do the laundry and make your clothes and cook for you magic folks. We do the garden and do all the repairs on the school."

"That doesn't sound like fun. It sounds like slavery," Alice replied.

"We are free to leave if we wish but it's our purpose Miss. It's the way it's always been. We stay out of the way as much as we can. We use secret passages in the walls so we don't get in the way and we know our place. That's why the ancestors made us, to serve you magical people, and everyone here is ever so kind."

"Wow! Secret passages – they sound cool!"

"They are sometimes quite chilly miss but a lot of the passages run behind fire places so they can warm up quite considerably," the girl replied naively.

"What's your first name?" Alice asked as they walked up the stairs together. She paused by the paintings of the former royal family.

"What happened to these people?" she asked.

"I don't know miss. They disappeared a long time ago then the council of Ethereals took over," she answered. They continued along a long corridor lined with more paintings and which had many doors.

"My folks call me Townie – Townie Thorne – that's my name."

"I'll call you Townie then," Alice said. "And you can call me Alice."

"Ooh - I don't know Miss," Townie replied hesitantly. "Well maybe when there's no one else around." They stopped outside a door on which was a brass plate containing the number 17. "Here's your room Miss – I'm sorry – Alice."

Townie opened the door and Alice walked in to the room. The room had two single beds, two wardrobes, a dressing table, a sink in one corner and a fireplace. There were cream blinds on the two windows but, to Alice's relief, no bars. Her blue suitcase and Justin Beiber poster were placed neatly at the foot of the bed nearest the fireplace.

"How did that get here before me?" Alice asked.

"I don't know Miss," Townie replied. "They don't tell me anything. Shall I unpack your bag?"

"No I'll do it," Alice felt uncomfortable; she was unused to being fussed over.

"Then I'll leave you to get settled in. The bell will sound when you need to come down to supper,"

Townie turned to leave. "You will need to get changed. Everything you will ever need will be in your wardrobe. They're magical."

"Well why wouldn't they be?" Alice shrugged sarcastically.

"Wait! Who's in the other bed?"

"That'll be your roommate – I'm not sure who they've put in here with you," Townie replied. Alice sighed. She'd shared rooms before in residential care and never liked it. Roommates got in your space and borrowed your stuff.

"Okay thanks Townie. I'm shattered I think I'll lie down," she said and lay down on the first bed. She took out her mobile phone and checked the screen.

"No signal – great," she said to herself. She put the phone away and closed her eyes. The bed was so comfortable she fell instantly asleep.

**

"Alice! Alice! Wake up!" a voice said. Alice felt someone shaking her. For a split second before she opened her eyes she imagined she'd wake to be in her pink room at her foster parent's home.

"What! Where am I?" she said, momentarily confused. A pretty, flaxen haired girl, with delicate facial features and green eyes, was sitting on the bed.

"Wake up silly or we're going to miss supper," the girl said. "Hi I'm Trudy Dragonsfoot. We're room mates." Alice sat up on the bed and looked at Trudy suspiciously.

"I'm Alice. Did you say something about supper?"

"Yes they told me your name when they assigned me this room," Trudy said with a smile. "Supper is in ten minutes and you need to wash and put your uniform on. It'll be in the wardrobe. The bathroom is through

37

there." She said pointing to a door Alice had not noticed before.

"Wow! En-suite rooms, that's smart!"

"I'll get changed while you shower. We have to wear full uniform to all meals. You'll find towels and everything else you need in the bathroom."

"Okay but don't touch my stuff," Alice replied.

The bathroom contained a bath, shower, hand basin, toilet and shelves for toiletries and had white tiles from floor to ceiling.

Alice washed quickly and returned to the bedroom where Trudy was waiting for her.

"So are you a genie too?" Alice asked Trudy.

"No, I'm a wood sprite. They didn't know where to put you. The genies are a bit bitchy and the warlocks are boys so they put you with me. We don't fit into any specific category. You're my first room mate," Trudy replied with a grin.

"What do wood sprites do?"

"We make flowers grow."

"I thought the elves look after natural things."

"They control larger forces, but, you'll learn all this in 'history and myth breaker' class. Anyway, can you hurry now? Get dressed." Alice noticed the fingers on the clock had not moved.

"I think the clock has stopped."

"Oh no, that was me. I stopped time so we wouldn't be late."

"You can do that as well? Lighthorne Herb did that on our journey here."

"It's a cheap trick. Most of us can do it but I can't hold it for long. Rather than time itself freezing, because that would affect the whole world, I think it just makes us move really fast so it seems like everything else is standing still. But I don't really know. Now hurry up and get dressed! Your clothes will be in the wardrobe."

Alice opened the wardrobe and pulled out the only clothes hanging within, a grey, ankle length skirt, a white, high collared blouse, and burgundy cardigan. These matched Trudy's uniform. There was also a pair of grey woollen tights and a pair of black lace up shoes. She took the clothes out of the wardrobe.

"I'll look like a granny if I put those on. What happens if I get this uniform dirty, there isn't anything else in there?"

"It's a magical wardrobe. Look! Close the door."

Alice dutifully closed the door.

"Party dress please!" Trudy said loudly. "Open the door again," she commanded Alice.

Alice opened the door to see a pink chiffon party dress with matching shoes and bag, hanging before her.

"It's your wardrobe. It knows what you need. Now can we please go and get supper? I am starving; you're not the only one who's had a long day."

"I hate this! I look like a geek!" Alice announced as she looked at her fully uniformed self in the long dressing mirror, which was on the back of the wardrobe door.

"What's a geek?" Trudy asked. Alice shook her head.

"You look very smart Miss," said the wardrobe. Alice did a double take.

"Thank you. It talks?" Alice asked Trudy.

"You'll get used to it. Now let's go down to the dining room."

Alice followed Trudy out of their shared room and along the corridor. Many other students were also making their way down for supper. Trudy briefly nodded to a couple of other students and a boy ran to join them.

"Hello, I'm Barton Bean," he announced.

"Hi, I'm Alice. I'm new here," she replied.

"I know. Me and Trudy have already been here one term and they told us you were coming."

He was a short boy who only came up to Alice's shoulders. He was stockily built and had a round pleasant face with a smattering of freckles over his nose. He wore the male version of the school uniform – burgundy jumper over a white shirt, with grey, full length trousers.

"What are you?" Alice asked.

"Goblin!"

"And what do goblins do?" she pressed.

"Goblin stuff," he answered with a shrug.

When they reached the top of the staircase Alice saw that the stairs and hallway below were filled with literally hundreds of other students all waiting to enter the dining room. Alice began to feel nervous. She didn't want to lose track of Trudy and Barton but there were so many people. Most of whom were taller than Alice and were all wearing the same uniform.

"Order! Order! I need order please," a booming voice announced from somewhere below. The students became quieter. "Firstly, will students from South house please enter the dining room and find your seats."

Alice clung onto the banister as she was pushed aside by people trying to get passed her.

"Is it always this mad?" she shouted to Trudy.

"No, it's just that it's the first day of term and we haven't been given our supper times yet, and everyone has come out of their rooms at once."

"North house next please," boomed the voice.

As the students from North house filed down stairs and through the hall into the dining room, the crowd thinned out.

"East house! Form a line and take your places in the

dining room."

Half of the remaining students filed away leaving Alice with Trudy and Barton and the other children of West house standing on the stairs and in the hallway. Alice and her friends shuffled into a single file behind the remaining children – Trudy first, then Alice and Barton, and marched into the dining room.

The dining room was vast. There were four long trestle tables, each displaying a house flag. A blue flag for North, yellow for South, green for East house, and tangerine for West. Each table had elaborate place settings, enough to seat over two hundred students. At the far end of the dining room was a dais where the faculty sat. Alice noted Miss Goddessbloom in the centre, and Lighthorne Herb sitting to her right. Rosebay Thistledown sat second from end on the left.

"I wonder how she got here so quickly?" Alice asked herself. Rosebay was chatting to a mad looking woman who had what looked like – at least from their viewpoint at the back of the room – snakes for hair.

"Oh my God! Who is that weird looking woman?" Alice asked.

"Who?" Barton asked.

"The woman talking to Rosebay Thistledown."

"Oh! That's Madame Inglenook Nightveil. She's the chemistry teacher."

"Scary!" Alice said. Barton and Trudy nodded in agreement.

"She's a witch," Barton put in.

Alice, Trudy and Barton found seats together on West table, and in the instant they were seated skitters filled their mugs with steaming hot chocolate and placed selections of cakes in front of them. Alice wanted to tuck in immediately but everyone else was waiting politely for the final stragglers to sit down so she followed suit.

41

Miss Goddessbloom stood on the dais to address her audience and tapped her cane loudly on the floor.

"Children! May I have your attention please?" The room hushed. "Before we partake of our grand dining experience I would like to take this opportunity to thank the skitters for their tireless work." A round of applause spread across the room. "I would also like to welcome all our new students and trust their experience of Bonneville Goodhouse will be both educational and pleasurable. We try to create a home from home within these walls and I find it so gratifying to see returning children from some of the oldest magical families, and children from some of the youngest families.

Now without further ado please – begin your meals." Rapturous applause echoed around the walls.

"This is already better than any of my foster homes," Alice said excitedly as she took a sip of her hot chocolate. "Oh my God! That chocolate is amazing! I've never tasted anything so good! It's like heaven in a mug."

"Wait till we start lessons – then make up your mind," Trudy replied as she bit into a lemon sizzle cake. "Neither Barton nor I are academic and we struggle to keep up with the other kids. It's hard work. Do you like studying Alice?"

"Don't know. I'm average I suppose," she replied thoughtfully.

"I think I'm going to die from a sugar overdose!" Barton exclaimed as he tucked into his third iced topped cake.

"Do we get this every night?" Alice asked. Trudy shook her head.

"No, we usually only get toast and cereal in the evening, but as it's the first day of term tomorrow this is a treat to help the new people settle in," Trudy answered.

As soon as a plate or cup was used it was collected swiftly and silently by one of the skitters. Once everyone had finished eating, the tables were cleared completely.

The lights dimmed and with a creak and a groan from rusty cogs, the vaulted oak beam ceiling began to slowly open exposing the night's sky.

"What's happening?" Alice asked as she gazed at the open sky and stars above.

"Wait and see!" Trudy replied. Alice huffed. She was getting fed up of people saying that to her.

"Fireworks!" squealed Barton with delight.

A hundred rockets shot into the pitch black sky, bursting into a million, silver, purple, turquoise and red sparkling diamonds. Loud explosions boomed as each rocket shed its payload. A second volley followed the first. These created tangerine spirals in the air like giant chrysanthemum blooms, all joining to culminate in gold, sunflower shapes that hovered for seconds before dissipating.

The children gasped in awe and squealed with delight. Alice had never felt so happy. She had no idea what the future held but for the first time in her life she felt she was where she belonged.

When the firework show ended everyone clapped wildly. The lights came up and children groaned. The roof began to slowly close.

"That was amazing!" Alice exclaimed.

"Children! Children! Settle down please," Miss Goddessbloom ordered as her microphone screeched loudly with interference. "Breakfast will be served at 7am tomorrow morning. Lessons begin at 9am sharp. Your schedules will be in your rooms when you return. I suggest you all get a good night's sleep," she concluded: "You may now leave."

The children began filing out of the hall in an

orderly fashion. Once they reached room 17, Alice and Trudy bade farewell to Barton. He moved on to his own room – number 23, just down the corridor. Set out neatly on her bed Alice found a bag, a complicated looking rota and three books – A History of Magic Throughout Time by J.J. Tallbrick, Genies Through the Ages by Kareema Del Sol, and Myths and Mythology, The Truth by Musa Fixa. There were also empty note books, a pencil case containing pens, pencils, rulers and various other stationery items and mathematical equipment.

"I can't understand this," Alice said with exasperation as she looked at the rota. Trudy glanced at it.

"Don't worry. It looks like we're in most of the same classes tomorrow so we can go together. "You'll get the hang of it."

Alice moved the books and stationery off her bed and got undressed, putting on a pink nightdress she had brought with her from her foster home, and carefully hung her uniform back into the wardrobe.

"Thank you!" the wardrobe said.

"That's creepy," she said. Trudy smiled as she climbed into her own bed.

"You'll get used to it. Good night Alice."

Alice brushed her teeth then climbed into bed.

"This is like – unreal. I will never sleep! Yesterday I woke up in my foster parents' house. Today I woke up in a hotel and was brought here on a whale, by some crazy guy with a crazy story. Tonight I'm going to sleep in a room with a talking wardrobe. Good night Trudy. See you tomorrow." She instantly fell fast asleep.

Chapter Seven

The next morning the school wake up alarm rang at 6.45am. Alice groaned in her bed.

"It feels like I just went to bed – I'm still tired," she said.

"I'll take the first shower," said Trudy as she slipped out of bed. Alice closed her eyes once more and the events of the previous day flashed through her mind. The fin whales – the fireworks display – the magical wardrobe. Suddenly she was wide awake.

"This is awesome," she shouted as Trudy emerged from the shower. "I can't believe this is really happening!"

Alice showered and dressed in a new, clean uniform provided by the wardrobe and the girls headed downstairs. The hallway was not as manic as it had been the previous evening, as the buffet style breakfast was served over an hour and a half period and students could come and go as they pleased.

She helped herself to three croissants, fruit juice, tea, a bowl of porridge and four slices of toast. They found seats close to main door.

"Wow! You eat as much as Barton," Trudy said, as she examined Alice's selection. Trudy simply had a bowl of cereal and a cup of tea.

"When you grow up in care you learn to help yourself to whatever is available," Alice replied. "You have to take what you can get." She wrapped the croissants in a napkin and put them in her pocket. Trudy winced.

"Sorry Alice, I forgot you grew up in the human world," she said. "Is it really bad?"

"No, not really. Some times I was placed with foster carers. Most of them were okay, there's just no stability.

You get passed from place to place," Alice replied sadly. "What about you? Got any family?"

"There are many of us – hundreds maybe – and we're all related, but I'm the first to come here. "Wood sprites have to move into the 21st century". That's what the Grand Master said when my parents decided to send me here. He's the ruler of the wood sprites.

There are different colonies of wood sprites all over the world but I'm from the forest of Dhuridhin on the other side of the island."

"Dhuridhin?"

"Yes, Hy Brasil is split into two kingdoms. I don't know what happened to the kings or the royal families but there are some pictures of them in the main hall. They haven't been around for hundreds of years. Firstly there's Lightwold which is where we are. It consists of the school, the docks where you landed, farms and Lightwold town. Then there is Dhuridhin beyond the mountains – which has another town, a castle, more farms and the forest where I live."

"The island must be huge! It's amazing the humans haven't found it."

"Magic!" Barton announced as he sat down beside them with his tray overflowing with bagels, buns, croissants and what looked like a chocolate rice pudding. He'd also helped himself to a milkshake, fruit juice, tea and coffee.

Three tall, beautiful dark skinned, black haired girls, glided passed the table where Alice, Trudy and Barton sat, knocking Barton's seat so he spilt his chocolate milkshake.

"Watch it fatty!" the leader said.

"It was your fault," Alice replied leaping to Barton's defence. The girls glared at Alice and moved on.

"Who the Hell do they think they are?" Alice said.

"You shouldn't have said anything Alice," Barton

replied. "They're the djinn – queen genies – very powerful." Alice shrugged. "Eloise, Avuncnia and Plasadera. They can do stuff like turn you into a statue or make you disappear altogether."

"Well I'm a genie too so maybe I can do all that stuff."

"I told you yesterday the other genies are really nasty, but the way I heard it, one day you'll be more powerful than any of them," Trudy put in. "For now though it's probably a good idea not to get on their bad side."

"Where did you here that about me?" Alice asked.

"Common knowledge," Barton said.

"It's weird. Everyone here seems to know something about me and yet I grew up in total ignorance. I knew nothing until Herb turned up."

After breakfast Alice and Trudy packed their black school bags with the books and stationery items provided for them and they, together with Barton made their way to the first classroom marked on their rota for a History of Magic lesson.

"Beans, Devises and Dragonsfoot," commanded a lanky boy wearing a graduate's cloak. "You're first alphabetically – take the first three desks please. "Elfin, Folliage, Igloohouse….," he continued, three other students stepped forward. Alice, Barton and Trudy took their seats. Alice looked around. The walls were panelled in dark oak, the ceilings were high and through the stone arch windows she could see the five giant heads: Uhh, Ba Guh, Ba, Ba on the lawn at the front of the school, still rising and falling in turn.

"Maybe the rooms are assigned alphabetically as well," Barton mused. "That's why our rooms are so close to each other."

"Possibly. Who's the tall, bossy guy? Is he the teacher?" Alice asked.

"No, he's Marcus Primus, a Perfect," Trudy replied.

"You mean prefect," Alice corrected.

"No, teaching assistants are called Perfects. They have to be perfect in every aspect of their behaviour and study," Trudy answered.

"I guess I'll never be one of them then," Alice joked.

"Sit down! Sit down! Everybody sit down and stop talking!" demanded a voice from the head of the room. The students all sat obediently at their assigned wooden desks. Alice craned her neck to see who was talking. The voice came from a short man who looked, and was dressed like a garden gnome, complete with a red pointed hat with a bell on the end. "I am Master Tallbrick. Mr Primus – please write my name on the blackboard."

"So much for the 21st century," Alice whispered under her breath.

"You have a comment Miss Devises?" Tallbrick asked. *How did he hear what I said,* she thought, *it must be the big ears?*

"Sorry, it's just that most schools in the real world use white boards and markers and have computers. Black boards and chalk are like, really old."

"So – the real world – like," he sneered. "You are an authority on education then are you? Can teachers in 'the real world' do this?" He snapped his fingers and every window in the classroom opened and then shut again. All the books and bags in the room floated to the ceiling, then, returned to their original places.

"No – sorry. I'll keep my mouth shut," said Alice, duly admonished.

"Very well. You are new to Bonneville Goodhouse so I'll let this infraction go. Be careful in future."

Drama queen, she thought.

"I can also read minds Miss Devises!"

A History of Magic – Part One, it read on the board.

Alice noticed the other children were starting to take notes as Master Tallbrick spoke, so she followed suit.

"Turn to page one of your History of Magic text book please," Tallbrick announced. "Magic has been around since the beginning of time. It works in conjunction with the sciences, but paradoxically can also be defined as anti-physics – defying the laws of nature!"

Alice realised he was purely, monotonously reciting the words from the book and decided it was easier to read than listen to Tallbrick. His voice was so boring.

An hour later a bell sounded to end the lesson. The class breathed a sigh of relief. Alice was disappointed. She'd hoped to see examples of how to use magic rather than simply listening to Tallbrick drone on about history. The pupils began to file out of the classroom and Alice moved to follow Trudy.

"Miss Devises – a word please," Tallbrick said. *Oh no, what have I done now,* she thought?

"Nothing – you've done nothing wrong," he continued. Alice stood silently as the last of her classmates left the room. "Miss Devises – I was a friend to both your parents. We grew up together – many – many years ago. If you ever need any help I would be happy to offer you assistance."

"Wow, everyone is so nice here," she replied. Tallbrick inhaled deeply.

"I hope that remains the case. Now get on to your next class."

"Thank you – sir," she said hesitantly as she left to join Trudy and Barton who were waiting for her in the corridor outside the classroom.

The children had different classes for second period and so had to go their separate ways. Trudy and Barton showed Alice where her classroom was before they moved on to their own. She didn't want to leave them but, nervously clutching her bag in front of her, she entered room 33.3 Elemental Physics.

**

The classroom was more akin to an Arabian boudoir than physics lab. Sumptuous gold, magenta and tangerine bolts of satin draped across the ceiling from the centre golden chandelier, to the edges of the room. It was a large room with no desks or chairs, instead large, luxurious cushions and plush multicoloured rugs covered the polished marble floor.

A tall, beautiful blonde lady smiled as Alice entered the room.

"You must be Alice!" she declared. "I am Farzeena Del Sol."

"Teacher or Perfect?" Alice asked. Farzeena laughed musically.

"Why, I'm the teacher you dear, sweet girl."

"Did you write the book for this lesson?" Alice asked, envisioning another boring lesson spent simply following the words in a text book.

"No dear," Farzeena replied sweetly, "that was my sister, and I don't do books. They're boring."

"Sounds good," Alice said with a smile. Alice looked around at the other students. Instead of wearing school uniform they were all dressed in bright, exotic costumes. The boys wore pantaloons with gold waistcoats while the girls wore chiffon harem pants with a chorli, a short blouse, and light veils attached to their hair. She instantly felt at home.

"Sorry," Alice said quietly. "I didn't realise I had to get changed."

"No," Farzeena whispered and briefly raised the index finger of her right hands to her lips. "We change in secret. The room is shielded. No one outside can see us. The squares don't approve." She snapped her fingers and Alice's clothes were replaced with a scarlet pants suit. "If you don't like the colour, change it yourself."

"Snap my fingers?" she asked.

"Snap your fingers, wiggle your nose, blink your eyes, or tap your toes," Farzeena sang with a smile. Alice clicked her fingers and her harem pants suit changed from scarlet to turquoise. "Excellent darling! Now let me introduce you to the rest of the class.

These are Adham, Shakil, and Kareem," she said pointing to three older boys lounging at the back of the room. "This is Eloise, Avuncnia and Plasadera, they are my Perfects." The older girls glided across the room towards her. It seemed as if they floated, barely touching the floor at all. These were the girls she'd seen at breakfast in the dining room.

"Welcome Alice," they sang in unison. "You're one of us now."

"And this is Sherzeen and Sheharazade," Farzeena continued. Alice made herself comfortable on a large violet floor cushion between the two girls. "They are also new to the class.

Today, you new children will be practising flying carpet levitation. Please take a carpet," she pointed to a pile of small rugs at the front of the room. "The Perfects will guide you through it. Meanwhile, you boys practice the shrinking assignment I set you over the summer."

This is more like it! Alice thought. *Real magic!*

Plasadera joined Alice, while Avuncnia and Eloise moved to assist Sherzeen and Sheharazade. Alice picked a rug off the top of the pile, it was heavier than it looked and she placed it on the floor next to the other two new girl's rugs.

"There are many ways of travelling on carpets,"

Farzeena said. "It is easier to sit cross legged or to kneel but today I'd like you to perfect simple hovering while you stand on the carpet."

"Step onto the carpet and face me," Plasadera said softly. Alice did as she was told. "Take my hand and focus on your balance."

"My balance?" Alice asked. She took Plasadera's hand to steady herself.

"Yes," Plasadera replied. "It is not the carpet that is magic Alice, but, it is your thoughts that will make it fly. Now – concentrate. Just think – arise! "

Alice closed her eyes and whispered, "RISE!" She opened one eye and wrinkled her nose - nothing happened. The disappointment stung.

"Try again," Plasadera said patiently.

"RISE!" Alice repeated. Still nothing happened. She opened both eyes and noticed that Sherzeen and Sheharazade were gracefully hovering on their carpets, being steadied by their Perfects, a few inches above the ground.

"RISE NOW!" she said firmly and the rug beneath her feet shot into the air, throwing her backwards. Luckily, Plasadera still held her by the hand so she landed on her bottom, not her head.

"Damn it!" she exclaimed. Plasadera smiled.

"Don't worry; you've made a good start."

Alice spent the remainder of the lesson rising from the floor on the carpet and then falling off it. Plasadera was remarkably patient with her. When the lunch bell sounded Alice was disappointed the lesson was over. Farzeena returned the classroom to its original form and the students flashed back in to their school uniforms.

"Join us for lunch Alice!" Eloise said as they all headed out of the classroom. "We eat together. You're one of us now."

"Umm," she hesitated. "I'm supposed to meet my friends."

"Very well," said Avuncnia pleasantly. "It's your choice."

Her djinn classmates headed off together leaving Alice standing in the corridor alone. She looked for Trudy and Barton but couldn't find them.

The corridor slowly emptied of students and Alice began to regret letting the other djinn go without her.

"Alice," said a voice behind her. She turned sharply but saw no one. The corridor was badly lit, and without the babble of other children seemed oppressive and claustrophobic.

When she heard her name called once more from the empty corridor, she ran in the opposite direction.

Chapter Eight

Alice found Trudy and Barton in the dining room.

"This school is weird!" she said as she sat down on a seat they'd saved for her. "I swear, upstairs, I heard someone saying my name when there was no one else in the corridor." Barton shrugged.

"It could have been any number of things," Trudy said.

"Ghosts, demons, poltergeists," Barton put in.

"There's no such thing," Alice said. Her eyes widened. "Wait! All those things are real?"

"Of course!" Trudy replied. "And not all of them are friendly so it's best not to talk to them."

Alice shuffled nervously in her seat.

"Ghosts! That's scary, dead people – yuck! I'll try not to have anything to do with them," she said. Alice and Trudy tucked into a salad with new potatoes while Barton gorged on lamb stew and dumplings. "By the way, I've just had a class with the 'queen genies' and they're all lovely. They invited me to have lunch with them but I said I was meeting you."

"They would be nice to you because you're one of them, but they look down their noses at everyone else," Barton said.

"We have sport this afternoon," Trudy laughed. "That should help you burn off some of those calories Barton."

"I didn't get a sports kit," Alice said.

"Check your bag!" said Trudy. Alice looked into her bag and noticed her text books had disappeared to be replaced by a brand new sports outfit. "The bag is an extension of the wardrobe. It always knows what you need."

After lunch they followed their classmates to the

sports hall, a large building behind the main school.

"The boys' changing room is to the left, girls to the right. Get changed into your sports kit as quickly as you can children," said a large Amazonian, blonde woman. "I am Miss Saturnia and today we will be learning how to play lacrosse. When you're ready join me outside."

As soon as Alice and Trudy were changed they followed the other children and helped themselves to a lacrosse stick, which was about a metre long with a triangular shaped net at the end. They marched outside once more, to the lacrosse field. Alice had never heard of a sport called lacrosse. Having only attended inner city schools before, to Alice, the pitch looked huge. It was about 60 metres wide and 100 metres long. A midfield line divided the length of the field in half.

"I want two teams of ten." Alice, Trudy and Barton joined seven other students to form a team. Miss Saturnia handed out position jerseys. "You're in goal Barton, I doubt if anything will get passed you," she said, he nodded in agreement and ran down the field to take his position in the goal mouth. The goal measured about six feet high by six feet wide. "Trudy, Alice Devises – you're too small for attack or defence so make yourselves useful midfield."

Miss Saturnia briefly explained the rules to the students and showed them where to stand on the pitch. Alice listened to the teacher and got the gist of the game, *'blah, blah, blah, score more than your opponents'*, she thought, it seemed fairly straightforward.

"You catch and pass the ball using the net at the end of your lacrosse stick. The difference between the way we play lacrosse, and the way it is played in the human world, is that we can use magic. However, the use of magic in the 'attack area' in front of the goal keepers is forbidden." They took their positions and Miss Saturnia blew a whistle to start the game. The students took Miss Saturnia at her word and caught and passed the small rubber ball using levitation and occasional time freezes. Alice became frustrated. Each time she attempted to challenge an opponent they'd blink out of sight and materialise behind her.

"This is stupid!" she exclaimed fifteen minutes later as she sat in the middle of the pitch.

"This is an exercise in use of magic skills Miss Devises, as well as sport. I suggest you try harder," said Miss Saturnia.

Alice charged angrily at an opponent midfielder who had the ball and tackled him, before he could blink out of sight, knocking him to the ground. She took hold of the ball in the net at the top of her lacrosse stick, and bolted down the field ignoring her team mates' calls for her to pass to them, and also ignoring Miss Saturnia, who was madly blowing her whistle.

"Shoot! Shoot!" her friends called as she crossed the attack area. But she ignored them and she barged passed the opposing goalie knocking him out of the way, and then ran across the goal line with the ball still in her net.

"Yay! I've scored!" she screamed loudly and jumped up and down in triumph.

"Goal disallowed!" said Miss Saturnia. "You fouled an opposing player Miss Devises. I had blown my whistle to stop the game, Goal disallowed."

"That stinks! I did what you said. I scored a bloody goal!"

"You're out! Devises sit on the sidelines."

"Screw you!" Alice whispered under her breath.

"I heard that Devises," said Miss Saturnia angrily. "Now get off the field."

First day of term and I'm already in trouble, she thought to herself as she left the pitch, *I don't care. Let them throw me out, with my new powers I could rule any normal school.*

Secretly Alice hoped she wouldn't be in any real trouble. She watched the rest of the game wishing she could join in again, but Miss Saturnia ignored her completely.

Almost an hour later, Miss Saturnia blew her whistle to signal the end of the lesson. She ordered the children to return to return their equipment to the sport equipment cupboard and to shower and change into their day clothes. Trudy and Barton and the other children walked back to the changing rooms together giggling and chatting about the game. Alice followed at the rear feeling totally isolated, no one spoke to her.

"Aren't you going to shower?" Veronica Igloohouse - a girl to whom Alice had not previously spoken – asked when she noticed Alice quickly changing out of her sports clothes and back into her school uniform.

"I showered this morning and I didn't have time in the lesson to get sweaty," Alice replied resentfully. "And anyway, what's it got to do with you?"

"Fine – nothing – if you want to smell all day," Veronica snapped spitefully.

"Just shut your face or I'll shut it for you!" Alice replied. "Trudy, I'll wait for you outside." Trudy nodded in agreement. Alice shoved all her sports gear into her bag and stormed angrily out of the changing rooms.

Final period of the day was Potions, Lotions and Chemistry with Madame Inglenook Nightveil – the tutor Alice had seen Rosebay chatting to the previous evening. Up close, Alice saw that there were no actual snakes in Mme Nightveil's hair. Instead, her hair was made up of multi coloured dreadlocks, some of which stood up on top of her head, others jutted out at the side. Mme Nightveil's face was pale and gaunt and Alice thought her eyes looked cold and soulless.

The chemistry lab was a bright room with large window that let in plenty of daylight. It was filled with glass vials and Bunsen burners and jars full of pickled creatures. Mme Nightveil glared at Alice as she clambered onto a wooden stool between Barton and Trudy.

"I see we have some new faces in our midst!" Mme Nightveil announced loudly. "Well I am Mme Nightveil and this is my Perfect Tumbleena. She is my daughter." Alice sniggered and whispered to Barton;

"I believe that is called nepotism."

"You!" Mme Nightveil pointed to Alice. "Stand up and tell me about yourself." Alice rose awkwardly to her feet.

"What's the matter?" Mme Nightveil said. Alice shrugged. "Cat got your tongue?"

Out of nowhere a large black cat appeared and launched itself at Alice's face. The class screamed and scattered. Alice froze in horror as the virtual cat passed through her leaving her hair standing on end. Mme Nightveil shrieked with laughter.

"I'm sorry Miss Devices," Mme Nightveil giggled. "Just my idea of humour. You shouldn't have laughed at my daughter's name."

"That was horrible!" Alice screamed.

"Oh lighten up," said Mme Nightveil. "I like to start with an icebreaker. Today you're it."

Alice's heart was racing in her chest as she sat back down in her seat.

"Sorry," Barton whispered. "We should have warned you she's got a really weird sense of humour."

"It's okay," Alice replied. "You weren't to know she'd pick on me."

"Right Devises, stand up again," the teacher yelled across the room. "Tell me something – where does all your food come from?" Alice rose and shrugged.

"The kitchen," she replied. The other students laughed. Mme Nightveil sighed.

"I dearly hope that your answer is not representative of the British education system."

"What?"

"Do you really not know where food comes from?"

"Yeah course I do – supermarkets." The students laughed.

"That's enough!" Mme Nightveil snapped. "Sit down Alice! The food you eat – the clothes on your back – everything in the universe is composed of elements that cannot be created or destroyed. No matter how powerful or magical you are – anything you manifest has to draw the chemical elements from the universe," she tapped the desk in front of her and a large chocolate cake appeared. "You all may believe I simply conjured this cake but in truth the ingredients had to be produced. The cocoa, sugar and flour had to be grown. The butter was produced from cows' milk – the eggs were produced by hens. We draw these elements together but we create nothing.

Now let us get on."

Mme Nightveil ordered them to put on goggles and white coats and they spent the lesson measuring liquids and mixing colourful powders and crystals supervised by the Perfect. Thankfully Mme Nightveil played no more tricks on Alice but she remained on edge for the remainder of the lesson.

**

Later that evening, after supper, Barton joined Trudy and Alice in their room.

"What you did today on the lacrosse pitch was not cool Alice!" Barton said.

"God! I didn't mean anything by it. I just thought the game was boring so I decided to make it more fun."

"Like Mme Nightveil did. Let's hope Miss Saturnia doesn't make a fuss about it," said Trudy.

"I didn't do anything! What about what Mme Nightveil did to me?"

"That was funny. But you were a bit disrespectful to Miss Saturnia," Barton added.

"How?" she demanded.

"You swore in front of a teacher. No one ever talks back to teachers, it's just not done," said Trudy. Alice slumped on her bed.

"Well you goody, goody, boarding school brats, it's about time someone did!" her mind kicked into defence mode. "Maybe this isn't the place for me. Maybe I'd be better off going back to the real world. At least I'd be able to get a signal on my phone."

"Don't say that! I want us to be great friends – forever," Trudy squealed.

"BFFs," Alice laughed.

"I don't know what that means," Barton put in.

"God! You people are so backwards. It means best friends forever."

"Let's make a pact," said Trudy as she put out her right hand. Barton placed his right hand on top of Trudy's. "Come on Alice!" Alice reluctantly got off her bed and joined them. She placed her right hand on Barton's.

"BFFs FOREVER!" they shouted in unison and laughed. A knock came at the door.

"Maybe we're making too much noise," said Trudy as she opened the door. It was Townie, the little skitter maid.

"Hi Townie, do you want to join our best friends forever, forever gang?" Alice asked. Townie smiled.

"Master Lighthorne Herb has requested you come to

his study immediately," she said. "I'll show you the way." Alice, Barton and Trudy looked at each other nervously.

"You'd better go," Barton said. Alice nodded.

"And Mr Beans it's a bit late for you to be in the girls' bedroom. I think you should leave now," Townie added.

Barton and Alice said good night to Trudy and followed Townie along the corridor. They said goodbye when Barton reached his own room.

"Do you know why he wants to see me?" Alice asked. Townie shook her head.

"They don't tell me anything Miss," she replied.

"I meant what I said Townie – you could be part of our gang and hang out with us." Townie smiled.

"Thank you so much Miss Alice. I would love to but 'The Powers That Be' would never allow it. It's just not done."

"We'll just be friends in secret then," Alice said. Townie grinned. This was the happiest day of Townie's life. She'd never had a magical friend. The students were mostly indifferent to her and treated her as if she was invisible. But Alice wasn't like the others.

Townie led Alice to the corridor where the Masters' rooms were situated and knocked on Herb's large oak, study door.

"Come in!"

Alice said goodbye to Townie and entered the study. It was exactly as she'd imagined it would be with piles of dusty books and ornaments, maps of various places on the walls and two large globes of the world. Herb sat behind a big wooden desk.

"Sit down Alice," he said. She sat herself down on a chair across the table from Herb. Her feet didn't quite reach the floor. "It's been a busy three days eh?" he stated with a smile. "Drinking chocolate?" he offered.

Alice nodded and took the cup that appeared on the table before her. "How are you settling in?"

"I'm okay. I kind of miss television but the food's good, though you could do with a McDonalds," she replied. "It's a bit of a nuisance having to go to the dining room for every meal, and I can't get a signal on my phone. And computers. What kind of freaky school doesn't have computers?"

"We don't need them," he answered with a shrug.

"Not even the internet?"

"No. Made any friends?" he asked.

"Yep!"

"Good, I'm glad to hear it. Now Alice I've had a report from Miss Saturnia that you were rather insolent to her today," he said.

"No I wasn't – I was just trying to make the game we were playing a bit more interesting," she replied. "The rules were stupid!"

"And that's your decision is it?" he asked. Alice shrugged. "Alice I want you to understand your position in this school. You are only one of almost eight hundred students. Each of them is equally as important as you."

"I thought I was a progeny."

"The progeny of two magical creatures, yes – not a prodigy. Look up the difference."

"I would if my phone was working or if I had a computer."

"Try using a book."

"Hey, you came for me remember? I could always go back."

"No, you can't!" he said forcefully. "We could never allow an untrained magical creature to roam freely in the human world."

"So I'm a prisoner?" she asked, becoming increasingly concerned. "Have you got dungeons where you can lock me up?"

"Yes – well no! We do have dungeons but we would never lock you up. What I mean is, you must learn to conform, or, I will have to order one-to-one tuition. You'd live alone, eat alone, be alone and not be allowed to mix with the other children. You cannot be allowed to disrupt the smooth running of classes or encourage disruptive behaviour with the other students. You would remain at the school, but not be part of it." Alice began to feel worried. She took a sip of her hot chocolate and gulped. "There is also the ongoing threat to you from Zephyr. He will know we have found you and should you ever return to the human world your life would be in danger." Seeing her concern he continued. "Look, it's only the beginning of term and you're still settling in, so don't worry. Just try not to be antagonistic with the teachers." She nodded.

"I'll try," she said quietly.

"Good. What do you think of the school so far?" Herb asked.

"I expected more magic. I mean everything should be magic, all the time," she replied.

"Take a look at this book," he said as he opened a large red book, which was on the desk in front of him. Alice stood up from her chair so she could see better. The pages looked blank, but as Alice watched, hand written script appeared on the paper.

"I can't read it – why does it look like it's been written by a spider, and what language is that?" she asked. Herb lifted the book and whispered:

"English version." The words on the pages changed to English.

"Turn around and look at the painting above the fireplace," Herb said. Alice turned around and looked at the picture. It was a portrait of a man who reminded Alice of an ancient Egyptian, he had black straight hair that looked like a wig and thick black makeup around his eyes. He was sitting at a desk, scribbling with a pen made from a swan's feather. She moved closer to the fireplace. The more she stared, the more real the painting became, giving it a 3D effect. The Egyptian looked as if he was actually writing on the ledger before him.

"That is Ptolemy. Since Ethereals came to this world he has been cataloguing every single thing that has happened, and is happening on Earth." Alice looked confused. "Do you see the volumes behind him?" Herb asked. Alice nodded. "That is the history of this world – past, present and possibly future. It has become increasingly hard for him since the explosion in the human population. To make things easier for Ptolemy we receive a copy of every new book that is written."

"Can I ask you something?" Alice asked. It was Herb's turn to nod. "If you people are so powerful – why do you let bad things happen? Like poverty and murder and wars!"

"I'm sorry; I've told you before Alice, we can't interfere with human affairs. No matter how much we want to. Who are we to take sides in wars? And there simply aren't enough of us to police the whole galaxy. Now, before we get side tracked, I want you to have a look at this book." He took a large leather bound book named Magnus Opus from the bookshelves. It had a picture of a weird mythological creature with three eyes and six legs, on the front cover. He opened it in front of Alice. "Choose a subject you'd like to research," he said.

"I don't know – how about dinosaurs," she replied. Herb nodded.

"Dinosaurs!" he commanded. A holographic image of a tyrannosaurus rex appeared above the blank pages of the book.

"Tyrannosaurus," said the book, "meaning 'tyrant lizard' – a bipedal dinosaur."

"Brachiosaurus!" Herb said. The image changed to one of a long necked dinosaur and the book began to give a definition. "See! We don't need computers or the internet. The Magnus Opus can help you with your studies and give you any information you need to know. The book draws on the history that Ptolemy has written. It can even tap into news networks around the world. Help yourself to a Magnus Opus from the library.

Now get off back to your room. It's time for bed. Tomorrow is another day – make a fresh start." He ushered her out of the study.

Townie was nowhere to be seen and Alice was unsure which way she should go. When she heard her name again, whispering down the corridor, she ran in the opposite direction.

**

Over the next few weeks Alice began to adjust to the discipline and her new life at the school. She tried to be obedient and stay out of trouble, never questioning the teachers, even when she thought they were wrong. She apologised to Miss Saturnia for her behaviour on the lacrosse pitch and promised it would never happen again. Having Trudy and Barton as friends helped, as, whenever she committed a faux pas, they'd give her a nudge or a wink and she could apologise or rectify her mistake. She struggled with ancient Gaelic and ancient Greek classes and questioned the relevance of learning such archaic languages. Master Voltaire, the languages lecturer, explained that though English is very useful, there are other parts of the Ethereal universe that use more ancient languages. Alice excelled in art, cookery,

English and drama but she disliked maths and science, even though they all kind of made sense.

Alice spent many hours with a Magnus Opus book, trying to find out the latest celebrity gossip, what her hero, Justin Beiber, was up to and what was happening on Glee and Holly Oaks. The Magnus Opus, however, frequently reminded her that it was only to be used for serious research and not to be used for trivia. But occasionally, just for fun, it gave her a glimpse of the latest outrageous celeb antics. What she really loved were her lessons with the djinn. They were always light hearted and a welcome relief from the overbearing restraint Alice had to exercise at other times. Farzeena Del Sol was more like a friend who treated her students as equals unlike any of the other teachers

Chapter Nine

One warm Sunday morning at the beginning of half term week, in late October Alice, Trudy and Barton took advantage of the autumn sunshine and went out onto the front lawn for a picnic. A myriad of golden and scarlet leaves, as big as sheets of A4 paper, cascaded from the trees, and were swirled into loose piles by the cool west wind. Trudy collected a basket of fruit, bread and jam from the kitchen, Alice brought a bottle of lemonade she'd put aside at breakfast and Barton brought a coffee sponge cake his mother had sent from home. They laid a blanket on the grass and shared out their food equally.

The lawn was filled with pockets of students, some playing games, others reading and some practising their magic skills. Alice looked up into the clear blue sky and watched the vapour trails left by two planes dissipate in the upper atmosphere.

"It's funny, no one on those planes can see us or the island, yet we can see them," Alice said wistfully.

"That's magic for you," Barton replied.

"I don't like this time of year," Trudy said sadly. "All the plants go to sleep for the winter. Spring is the best time."

"I love all the seasons," Alice said as she lay back on the blanket. She chewed on the stalk of a long blade of grass. "The way the trees change colour in autumn is beautiful. What about you Barton? What's your favourite time of year?"

"Christmas I suppose. We have the winter solstice festival, and Saint Nicolas comes and brings us presents. I can't wait to go home for the winter holidays. I'm fed up of having to work so hard."

"Saint Nicolas?" Alice asked.

"Humans call him Father Christmas," said Trudy.

"Wow! He actually comes here?"

"Yep!" Trudy and Barton said in unison.

"That is AWESOME! Wait a minute – if you're not Christians why do you celebrate Christmas."

"Our people have been celebrating mid winter for thousands of years – pre dating Christianity. The dates just happen to coincide and St Nicholas is one of us," said Trudy.

"St Nicholas is a wood sprite?" Alice asked.

"No," said Barton. "I think he's an elf but I'm not sure so don't quote me on it."

"We've got the All Hallows festival at the end of this week," said Trudy.

"That's Halloween isn't it? Do we go trick or treating?" Alice asked.

"No, but we do have a party," Trudy replied. "Apparently, I heard, the genies don't usually show up. It's more for the witches and warlocks."

"Why's that?" Alice asked. Trudy and Barton shrugged.

"Don't know – maybe the genies think it's too pagan," said Trudy.

"They don't like the cold nights. Maybe All Hallows Eve is just too cold for them," said Barton. "Anyway I'm going to miss it. My mum wants me to go home for a couple of days."

**

Alice was first to hear the commotion.

"What's that?" Barton asked. They all stood up to see a crowd of laughing children surrounding the giant heads. Alice, Barton and Trudy moved forward and pushed through the crowd until they could see what the fuss was about.

Alice saw her friend Townie perched precariously on top of the Uhh, the first giant head, Uhh was at its lowest point, about eight feet off the ground. The heads continued to rise and sink in order. Townie screamed as Uhh began to rise. A group of five, senior year warlocks, all wearing long black cloaks over their school uniform, stood in a circle around Uhh laughing at Townie's cries.

"What the Hell is going on?" Alice asked the first warlock.

"Just having some fun, pipsqueak! What's it got to do with you?" he snarled back at her.

"What is this – the 1950s? I don't believe you people. Pipsqueak is a stupid word: you bunch of boarding school idiots. No one uses words like that any more. Get her down! She's my friend," Alice demanded. The warlock moved towards her and pushed her to the ground.

"You think you're tough don't you? Just because you grew up in the human world. She's only a skitter. Want to join her?" said a second boy.

"Help me Miss Alice, please!" Townie cried as Uhh began to descend once more.

"That's enough!" Alice said as she rose to her feet. "Out of my way!" With a wave of her hands she threw all five warlocks to across the lawn and into the surrounding crowd of students. "Hang on Townie, I'm getting you down." She focused on Townie and as Uhh reached its lowest point once more, she concentrated and lifted Townie with her mind, and lowering her safely to the ground.

"Thank you so much Miss Alice," Townie said gratefully.

"You'd better stay away from those boys in future," Alice told her. Townie nodded. She dusted down her maid's uniform and ran off towards the school. Alice turned to the warlocks. "I'm not tough, but I'm more street smart than any of you – so back off!" Two of the warlocks were still on the ground nursing their injuries. The other three boys began running towards her. Without thought she raised her right arm forcefully and cast them backwards. They flew so high in the air that they landed in one of the beech trees that lined the road to Bonneville Goodhouse. "And don't call me pipsqueak," she called after them.

From her office window at the front of the school, Athena Goddessbloom watched the events unfolding on the lawn outside.

"Did you see that?" she said to Lighthorne Herb who stood behind her.

"I did," he replied.

"She's just floored five very powerful warlocks with just a wave of her hand."

"You could say she tree-ed them."

"It's not a joke Lighthorne. We may have to implement our plan sooner than we thought."

"She's still just a child Athena. We need to wait until she comes into her full powers."

"If we wait too long she may become uncontrollable. She's too powerful already. Zephyr will make his move soon."

**

The week's lessons were suspended for the festival of All Hallows Eve and half term. Barton was taking the opportunity to return to his home on the Irish mainland. Alice and Trudy wanted to explore the island and with permission, on the proviso that they returned for five o'clock in the afternoon, accompanied Barton to Lightwold town for him to catch a whale transport. As it was half term and they were going off school property, they were allowed to wear casual clothes. It was good to be out of school uniform but Alice and Trudy decided to wear matching jeans and trainers. Their wardrobes dutifully obliged and provided them with jeans, jumpers and outdoor coats. Alice drew the line when wardrobe gave her a matching hat, gloves and scarf set.

"It's not that cold outside wardrobe," Alice said as she replaced the items back into the wardrobe.

"There's a storm crossing the Atlantic Miss Alice. The weather can change in the blink of an eye."

"Thank you but I'm sure we'll be fine."

Trudy and Alice met up with Barton on the front steps, and boarded a buggy transport, with a number of other students, who were also travelling to the town.

"We're a bit early," Barton said when they arrived in Lightwold. "My whale hasn't come in yet. Shall we have a look around the shops?"

"We can do but I haven't got any money," Alice replied.

"You must have some credits by now," said Trudy.

"What are credits?"

"We get one credit a week just for turning up to school," Barton said. "Then we can spend them in the local shops. We can buy sweets or presents and stuff."

"You also get credits added for exceptional work or behaviour," Trudy added. "Let's go to the bank to see how much you have."

They walked arm in arm up a steep cobbled street towards the bank which was at the top of a hill. Large white and grey seagulls screeched overhead and the air smelled of fish and the salty sea.

The bank at the top of the hill was small and had none of the usual security features, such as cameras or bullet proof glass screens, which are found in a normal bank. It reminded Alice of an old Victorian shop like she'd seen in the movies, rather than a bank. The banker, a gnome with a long grey beard, grey suit, and grey, bowler hat, welcomed them, and pulled out a large leather bound ledger.

"Mr Beans, you have six credits," the banker read. Barton sighed. "Will you be wanting to spend them all today?"

"No I'll leave them for now. Maybe if I save up I'll have enough to get my mum a present in about ten years."

"What is your name young lady?"

"Alice Devises." He checked the ledger. "You have the grand total of nine credits."

"I'll take them," she said. From a drawer under his desk the banker drew a five credit note and four, one credit notes, then marked the withdrawal in the ledger. Alice took the credits from him and examined them curiously. *These notes could be easily forged,* she thought wickedly.

"I wouldn't be so sure of that Miss Devises," said the face on the five credit note. It was a picture of a king, and underneath his portrait it said *King Atlas XX.*

"Sorry," Alice said with amazement. She'd never seen money that could talk before, let alone money that could read your thoughts.

"Miss Dragonsfoot, I see you have fifty three credits." Alice and Barton raised their eyebrows at Trudy with surprise.

"What? I had twelve credits rolled over from last term. I'll take ten credits please Mr Banker," Alice and Barton glared at her again. "What? It's his name!" The banker smiled and nodded as he handed Trudy two five credit notes.

"Have a good day children," he said as they left the bank.

"All aboard! All aboard! The lovely Miss Ariel Finn

is docking. Anyone for transport to the mainland – please board now," came a shout from a Mer man on the dock.

"Quick – that's me – I'll have to run," said Barton frantically as he began to run down the uneven cobbled street.

"Don't panic Barton. Ariel won't go without you," said Trudy.

The children made their way to the dock as quickly as they could. They all hugged and said goodbye, and Barton climbed into the glass howdah on Ariel's back, joining two other Bonneville Goodhouse students who were also returning to the mainland. Ariel blew a fountain of water from her blow hole.

"I'll never get used to this place," Alice said wistfully as they watched Ariel set off to sea.

Alice and Trudy bought fish and chips from a small shop called Maive's Fave Plaice and sat on the dock to eat them. They dangled their legs over the edge of the sea wall. It was a chilly day and a cold wind blew off the sea, but the fish and chips were hot and delicious, and Alice thought she'd never been happier in her life. She had good friends and she'd found a place where she belonged.

"You look happy. Are you pleased Barton has gone away?" Trudy asked.

"No, Barton's great. It's just – I love it here! My life before this was – nothing. No love, no friendship, no sense of home. Always being moved from place to place. The school, the island, you, Barton. I love it all. I feel like I finally have someone to talk to and people that care about me."

"Let's have a look around the shops. I'd like to get a present for my mum and there's a little craft shop at the top of the hill that sells home made ornaments," said Trudy.

"Couldn't you just get wardrobe to make something?" Alice asked as she stood up to join Trudy.

"I'm not Barton!" Trudy laughed. "No I like to put a little thought into gifts for my mum. You'll have to meet her one day. She's lovely."

"I wish I'd known my mum," Alice said quietly.

"Oh I'm so sorry Alice I didn't mean to make you feel bad; I'd forgotten you lost your parents."

"That's okay Trudy, it's not your fault you've got a good family and I haven't."

"You can share them. My family welcomes everyone and they're all so loving and kind. Where are you going for the winter break?"

"That's at Christmas, isn't it? I hadn't really thought about it. I suppose I'll have to stay at the school."

"No! I insist you come home with me. I could never enjoy the holidays if you were all alone at the school."

"Well, if you're sure they won't mind, I think I'd like to go home with you."

"No problem. I'll just let mum know you're coming with me."

The town consisted of a row of shops which included the fish and chip shop, a fresh fish shop, a clothes and shoe shop, the bank, a greengrocers/butchers and the craft shop. There was a tackle and motor repair garage on the docks where the buggies and howdahs were stored. To the south of the town was a power plant that harnessed wind, wave and solar power to provide electricity to most of the island, including the school. There was also a small school for the children of the Mer people who lived in outlying houses surrounding the town.

The girls walked slowly back up the cobbled street to Kadeja's craft shop which was opposite the bank. Alice was happy to be out for the day. Even though she was enjoying the new life fate had delivered her, sometimes, she just longed to be out of the school. The craft shop was full of crystals and sweet smelling candles. Wind chimes hung in the window catching the sunlight and casting rainbow beams around the shop. After looking around and umming and ahhing over various candles and ornaments, Trudy bought her mother an eight inch tall, piece of fulgunite, which is fused quartz, created when sand is struck by lightning.

The lady in the shop was tall, with long silvery hair. She wore a long blue embroidered dress with trailing sleeves, and reminded Alice of Rosebay Thistledown. She looked at Alice carefully as Trudy made her purchase.

"You're djinn aren't you?" the lady said. Alice eyed her suspiciously.

"How do you know?" she asked.

"I am Kadeja, I am elfin. I can read people," the lady replied with a smile. "Tell me ladies how are you getting back to the school?"

"We'll catch a buggy transport," Trudy replied.

"Why don't you fly? You are djinn and I can sell you a magic carpet," Kadeja said.

"I'm not ready, I've only practised levitation so far, and I'm not very good at it," Alice said, but she was sorely tempted. The djinn lessons were more relaxed than most but she sometimes she yearned to take control of her own magic. Kadeja pulled a carpet out from under the counter.

"How much is it?" Alice asked tentatively.

"How much do you have?" Kadeja said.

"I have eight credits left," Alice replied. She had spent one credit on her fish and chips lunch.

"Then the price of the carpet is eight credits," Kadeja said.

"Okay – I don't think I'll need any more money today."

"Alice, no!" Trudy said with concern. Kadeja cast Trudy an angry glance.

"Come on Trudy it'll be fun, and I have been practising every week since the start of term," said Alice excitedly. Trudy was worried, but Alice's enthusiasm was contagious.

"But we'll get into trouble," Trudy protested half heartedly.

"Why? Are there any rules against it? We were told to be back by five o'clock – no one said how we should get back."

"I'm scared," said Trudy. "I don't think we should."

"Look, you get a buggy back to the school if you like, but I'm going to fly," Alice replied.

Alice handed Kadeja eight credits in exchange for the carpet.

"Perhaps you'd like to practise out the back of the shop before you take off," Kadeja suggested with a grin.

"No, it'll be fine," Alice said confidently. Trudy sighed.

Outside the shop Alice and Trudy slipped into a secluded alleyway and unfurled the carpet on the ground. It was dark red with a multi-coloured pattern and looked like something you'd find in an old lady's house. The carpet was five feet in length and four feet wide – larger than the carpets she'd been practising on. Alice took a quick look around to make sure no one was watching, just in case the whole thing went wrong. She didn't want anyone to see if they fell off. She knelt on the carpet and closed her eyes. The carpet levitated and hovered about six inches above the ground.

"See! I can do it. It's easy," she exclaimed. "Get on if you're going to." Trudy hesitated but it did look as if it might be fun. She tentatively climbed on to the carpet behind Alice then lowered herself into a kneeling position.

"Right! Rise!" Alice commanded. The carpet with both girls on board rose slowly into the air until it cleared the top of the buildings. Trudy shrieked and grasped Alice tightly around the waist. Alice's heart pounded in her chest. She held the corners of the carpet so tightly her knuckles turned white.

"Forward!" Alice said forcefully hoping it would head towards school. The carpet shot forward so quickly the force pushed them both backwards. Trudy screamed. Alice screamed. The town disappeared behind them.

"I can't do this Alice! Put me down now!" Trudy yelled as a fly hit her in the eye.

"Wait! We'll be okay," Alice replied as she swallowed a large flying bug. She coughed, trying to clear her throat.

"I can't see. Put me down! NOW!" Trudy screamed.

"I'm not sure how to land. Hold on!" Alice shouted.

"What!"

"I haven't done the landing lesson yet!" she panicked.

Trudy squeezed Alice so hard she could barely breathe.

"You're holding on too tight! Let go of me! Carpet down!" Alice said firmly. The carpet ignored her and instead, gathered speed. The carpet turned and they flew in uncontrolled spirals back over the town, the docks, the power plant and the ocean. They rose so high that they could see the shore line of Achill Island and the village of Dooega in the distance.

"Aaargh!" they both screamed. Alice had no control. Around and around they span. They narrowly missed roofs, chimneys, a cockerel weather vane, the mast of a fishing boat and low flying seagulls, that seemed to be following them and mimicking their flight. Mer people in the town pointed in disbelief at the girls' uncontrolled antics. Alice and Trudy swirled up into the grey, wet clouds then swooped back down, almost into the water.

"We're going to die!" Trudy sobbed. "I don't want to drown. Get us over land!"

Alice closed her eyes as she was blasted by the sea wind and she concentrated with all her might. Her hair hit Trudy in the face.

"Get away from the ocean!" Alice ordered the carpet. It immediately did a 90 degree turn, almost unseating them, and headed inland. They flew once more over the docks and town and out into the open countryside. "Put us down!" The carpet came to a dead stop in the air above a field of cows, pitching them forwards but they managed to hold on. It began to rotate, slowly at first, then faster and faster.

"Whoa! I'm going to be sick!" Trudy screamed as the world spun around her.

"Down!" Alice cried. Finally, the carpet obeyed, and plummeted to the ground, crashing into the field below.

From her shop doorway Kadeja watched Alice and Trudy through an ancient, elaborately engraved, silver telescope. She laughed.

Alice had a cut on her forehead and Trudy's knees were grazed. Blood trickled into Alice's eyes. They were both covered in grass stains and mud, and Trudy was sure she'd landed in a cow pat.

"I'm so sorry Trudy, are you alright?" Alice cried. Trudy laughed.

"That was the most fun I've ever had," she shrieked.

"What? It was rubbish. Now we're going to have to walk back to town to get the transport. We could have been injured and we're filthy." Trudy rolled on the ground laughing.

"It was so funny," she squeaked, unable to draw a

breath. "I so want to do it again."

"Next time we wear goggles and crash helmets. My head is really hurting and I've failed. My ankle is killing me! This is supposed to be my destiny. I'm a genie – they fly on magic carpets! I'm such a loser."

They helped each other to stand, rolled up the carpet which had landed in a puddle of water, and headed for town.

"I'm in so much pain," Alice cried. "I think I've broken my ankle."

"Oh stop whining! It was your idea and you wouldn't be able be able to put any weight on your ankle at all if it was broken," said Trudy harshly, as she pulled twigs out of her hair. She gave Alice a tissue to hold against the cut on her forehead.

"I know but it really hurts."

Trudy checked that the fulgunite was still intact and put it safely into her pocket. Arm in arm Alice and Trudy limped back to Lightwold docks just in time to catch the last buggy transport.

"What happened to you two?" asked the Mer man driver.

"Nothing," Alice replied.

"We fell," said Trudy.

"Well, you smell like a farmyard," he said angrily. "I shouldn't really let you on board in that state."

"I'm sorry," said Alice weakly, "but can we please just go back to the school? I really need to see a nurse."

The Mer man sighed and started the buggy. "Okay but Miss Goddessbloom is going to hear about this," he said as he drove up the hill and out of town, towards the school. Trudy looked worried but Alice reassured her. The girls sat in the back of the buggy and hugged each other. Alice began to shake as the realisation of what she'd done sank in.

"Don't worry; I'll take the blame for everything. I'll

tell them I tricked you into coming with me," Alice said to Trudy. "No, we'll tell them I forced you."

Chapter Ten

"One communal buggy that needs fumigating," yelled Miss Goddessbloom the following morning. Alice and Trudy had both been summarily summoned to the headmistress' office. They stood silently in front of Miss Goddessbloom's desk. The girls' wounds had been dressed on their return to Bonneville Goodhouse the previous evening. Alice's forehead cut had needed a magical stitch, and had already healed well.

"Yes, we're sorry about that," Alice whispered under her breath.

"This week is a holiday for the skitters as well as the students. Can you tell me why their holiday should be disturbed just to clean up your mess?" The girls shrugged. "I should make you two clean the buggy."

"Sorry," they answered.

"Can't you just snap your fingers and make it clean again?" Alice put in. Miss Goddessbloom ignored her.

"One unauthorised flight over a populated area."

"Sorry," said Trudy meekly.

"What were you thinking? People, not just you two selfish girls, could have been injured. What if you'd fallen on someone? They could have been KILLED! A child – you could have killed a child!"

"Sorry," said Alice.

"Nurse Carbunkle had to be disturbed during her half term break to tend to your injuries. Can you tell me what gives you the right to take part in dangerous, unnecessary, unauthorised activities?"

"Sorry," Alice repeated. "It was my fault – I made Trudy come with me."

"So Miss Dragonsfoot – Miss Devises forced you, did she?" Miss Goddessbloom asked. Trudy nodded. "So she twisted your arm and threatened you with bodily injury if you did not accompany her."

"No – not exactly," Trudy whimpered.

"Then how exactly did she force you?" she yelled. Veins in her forehead started to protrude. Trudy was lost for words and began to cry.

"Go to your room Miss Dragonsfoot." Trudy attempted an uneasy curtsey and scuttled out of the office, still in tears. She felt miserable.

"Miss Devises – this is your last warning! If there is one more problem with you. Even the tiniest….."

"There won't ……"

"The tiniest infraction! I will separate you and Miss Dragonsfoot for good! I will put you on one-to-one probation. You will be isolated from the rest of the school. DO YOU UNDERSTAND ME?"

"Yes miss. I'm sorry."

"Where did you get the carpet?"

"Kadeja, the elfin lady in the craft shop in Lightwold, said I should buy the carpet and fly back to the school," Alice replied.

"Ahh! Kadeja is not an elf – she is a Trickster. She enjoys playing pranks and getting students into trouble."

"What's a Trickster?"

"Never you mind. I'll deal with her. Now get out of my office and remember what I said. This is your last warning!"

"Yes miss, sorry miss," Alice repeated as she attempted a bow and quickly backed out of the room.

In the dark panelled hallway outside Miss Goddessbloom's office, Alice lent against the wall and breathed a sigh of relief.

"Are you in trouble cos?" asked a tall, dark, older boy who Alice had never seen before.

"Who are you? I'm not your 'cos'."

"All djinn are family but I actually am your cousin.

Our mothers were sisters. I'm Sala'huddin. You can call me Al."

"What! We're really related? I don't believe it. Did you know my mother?" Alice asked excitedly.

"Yes, I remember her. I think I was around seven or eight, maybe nine, when she was killed," he replied. "Shall we get out of here so we can talk?" Alice nodded enthusiastically. He took her hand and she followed him across the main hall and into the dining room. Her heart beat roared loudly in her ears.

Sala'huddin collected two glasses of strawberry shortcake smoothies and they sat at an isolated table at the far end of the room.

"I can't believe it! I really have a family!" Alice exclaimed. "Why has no one told me? What's your mum like? Is she still alive? Where do you live? Do you have any brothers or sisters? Why did you never come for me?"

Sala'huddin laughed.

"Slow down! I remember you Alice – you were a really precocious brat, but we all loved you and we were devastated when you disappeared. My mum and your other aunties scoured the universe looking for you. They presumed Zephyr hadn't got hold of your powers because he would have tried to take over the Ethereals by now and there would have been all out war. So the aunts checked the runes every day and it was they who sensed your growing powers. During the battle –my mum knew Chloris was trying to send you to us in Istanbul, but we always supposed she was killed before she could complete the spell."

"I landed in Coventry in England," Alice said.

"Not quite as warm as Istanbul."

"No! I've never been able to stand the cold. Maybe that's the genie in me," Alice replied sadly. "So tell me about my family."

"You have three aunties, who all have three children. I have two older brothers. We live in the Middle East mainly, but since there have been so many human wars there lately we've been staying in Italy. I think my mum's in Hawaii."

"Can you take me to see them? I mean – do they want to meet me?"

"Yes and no. Yes, they do want you to join them, and no, the warlocks are fighting them for custody of you. Your dad was a warlock and his people don't want you to be with us. They want you with them.

Once we discovered where you were, there was some sort of big meeting of the clans, powwow, debate, confab, whatever, and it was decided you should stay at the school till you're old enough to make up your mind where you want to go."

"Don't I have a say in this?"

"No! Apparently not at the moment. My mum's sent me back here to keep an eye on you. Thanks for that, by the way. I thought I was done with this place. Now I've got to baby sit you."

"Sorry but I'm eleven not two. I don't need a baby sitter."

"It's okay. I don't mind. It gives me chance to hang out with my old mates."

"How come I haven't seen you here before?"

"Just got here."

"Tell me what it's like having a family."

"We're just like every other family I suppose. We fight and then we make up. But when we fight the earth shakes and storms happen."

"I want to meet them. I don't want anything to do with the stupid warlocks or this stupid school anymore. There are too many rules. I want to meet my family. Our family. I have a family," she squealed bouncing up and down with excitement.

"You will meet them. You've just got to be patient, that's all. Meanwhile, tonight is the All Hallows Eve party. It's a good laugh. You'll enjoy it."

"I thought the djinn didn't approve of pagan festivals."

"Hey – it's a party – no one can object to that."

Alice and her cousin talked for almost two hours. The time seemed to pass really quickly, until Sala'huddin excused himself to prepare for the evenings events. He walked Alice back to her room and kissed her on the cheek, promising to see her later.

**

"Trudy, Trudy, Trudy!" Alice screamed as she reached their shared room. "You'll never guess what's happened!"

"Miss Goddessbloom suspended you for your illegal flight."

"No, oh who cares about that? I've got a family and one of them is right here! I've got a cousin, and his name is Sala'huddin, but we can call him Al, and I've got a really big family that have been searching for me ever since I disappeared AND THEY WANT ME!." She bounced up and down on her bed.

"Slow down a second. Where have they been all this time? Why haven't you been told about them before?"

"I don't know," she said thoughtfully. "Maybe Miss Goddessbloom and Herb and every other teacher for that matter thought I didn't need to know. It is weird, they should have told me. But it doesn't matter now because I HAVE A FAMILY!"

That night the whole school and grounds were adorned with Halloween paraphernalia. Alice saw Herb and considered confronting him about how no one had told her about her family, but thought it best, for the time being, to not cause any more trouble. All the children donned fancy dress costumes. Wardrobe had provided Alice with a sparkling fairy outfit and Trudy dressed as a ghost.

A hundred pumpkin lanterns lined the path to a great bonfire in the centre of the front lawn. The skitters had prepared a hog roast with honey glazed baked potatoes and parsnips. There were candyfloss, pop corn and toffee apple stalls. Entertainers twirled glow poi into mesmerising swirls of colours and fire eaters juggled with swords and burning golden mesh balls.

As night fell Miss Goddessbloom lit the giant bonfire which sprang instantly into life.

"Enjoy yourselves children. But please do not go too near the fire," she shouted. The crowd roared with excitement. A steel drum band played rhythmically in the background as fireworks shot into the sky and exploded into a myriad of iridescent colours.

Athena Goddessbloom, Lighthorne Herb and Rosebay Thistledown sat together under a gazebo.

"You know the djinn have sent Sala'huddin back to watch Alice," Miss Goddessbloom said as she watched the festivities before her.

"Yes we will have to be careful, but while the djinn and warlocks are at each others' throats. We still have time," said Herb. He glanced at Rosebay.

"I agree," said Rosebay, "there's no point in making our move yet. We need to wait until she has all her powers."

Through the flickering flames of the bonfire Alice saw her cousin surrounded by Eloise, Avuncnia, Plasadera and the other djinn, all gazing lovingly at him. He mouthed something to Alice but she could not make out what he was saying.

"Is that your cousin with the djinn queens?" Trudy

asked. Alice nodded. "He's dreamy."

"Ahh he's not so good looking in daylight," Alice replied dismissively. Townie, dressed in a witches' costume, approached them carrying a tray of drinks.

"Would you like to try my mum's famous non alcoholic mead?" she asked proffering her tray towards Alice. Alice took the glass closest to her and took a sip of the liquid it contained.

"Oh my God! That is the best drink I've ever tasted!" she exclaimed. "It tastes like a summer's day and a starry night combined. What's in it?"

"Mainly honey and oranges," Townie said with a grin. "But my mum says the secret ingredient is love."

"Of course," Alice replied sarcastically. "What else would it be?"

"Nothing else miss?" Townie said innocently. The girls quickly finished their drinks and handed the glasses back to Townie.

Alice breathed in deeply and mistakenly inhaled a lung full of the smoke from the bonfire. She coughed violently. Her head began to spin. Alice stumbled as she watched one of the dancing entertainers, twirling his fire poi around and around in circles and spirals, hypnotically.

"Are you okay?" both Trudy and Townie asked simultaneously.

"Are you sure there's no booze in those drinks?" Alice asked. "I feel a bit dizzy."

"I'm sure," Townie replied firmly. "It is forbidden to give children alcohol."

"Maybe you should sit down," Trudy said. Alice looked pale.

"No I'll be fine; I just need to get away from the fire and the noise for a minute. You stay and have fun Trudy. I'll be okay." Alice walked away from the festivities. Her head span and she leant against the trunk of one of the great beech trees. An owl screeched overhead. Trudy joined a group of their classmates and disappeared from Alice's view. Even the stars in the sky seemed to be spinning. Alice closed her eyes and tried to straighten her thoughts but her mind still swam.

"Relax and sink into me," she heard these words in her head. Her body felt heavy and she sank backwards into the tree. It took just a moment. She felt life, coursing through the veins of the tree. "Sleep!" she heard in the mind. Alice opened her eyes and could see the yearly growth rings and flashes of the tree's experiences. It was like falling through time. Children in old fashioned dress climbing into the young tree's branches. A fleet of bi-planes flying overhead. Thousands of days and nights passing in a flash. The sun and the moon racing each other across the sky. It was as if there were hands on her shoulders pulling her backwards and down. It was crushing, enclosing her, enveloping her. She couldn't breathe. She could hear and see the All Hallows Eve festival no more. The world disappeared and she was completely immersed.

A stubby hand appeared before her face. She heard her name. She didn't want the hand to reach her. She wanted to stay and sleep forever, safely ensconced in the tree's sturdy walls.

"ALICE!" called a voice.

With one almighty jolt Alice was yanked out of the tree and back into the real world.

"Alice! Are you alright?"

"Master Tallbrick?" she said as she landed on the ground. She was confused. "I think that tree tried to eat me." Tallbrick nodded.

"That's one of Zephyr's old tricks. It wasn't the tree that sucked you in; rather it was Zephyr trying to absorb you."

"Where is he? Is he everywhere? I thought he'd

disappeared."

"No he's not everywhere but you must have ingested some wingot root. It's a powerful hallucinogenic. When you've been dosed with wingot root Zephyr is able to reach through the dimensional veil and take you. Have you eaten or drunk anything unusual?"

"Only the food at the festival. Trudy and I ate the same stuff though. So how come she wasn't affected?"

"Hmm," he said thoughtfully stroking his long grey beard. "I don't know. You must have been targeted specifically. I've told you before Alice, I was a good friend to your parents and I'd hate anything to happen to you."

"What can I do?" she asked, not really wanting to know the answer.

"Trust nobody!" said Tallbrick. He wanted to reassure her but knew that he alone could not keep her safe.

"Master Tallbrick – I met my cousin today. Why has no one told me I have a family?" Alice asked meekly.

"It's a long story my dear," he replied. He shook his head and stroked his beard. "But in short, Miss Goddessbloom thought it would be better if we let you adjust to school life before you were told. And her word is the law. We were instructed not to tell you."

"And you all went along with it? You – Herb – everyone! Well, you were wrong. You should have told me," Alice stated angrily. Tallbrick nodded in agreement.

"In hindsight – perhaps we should have told you."

They walked together back to the school. Alice felt too unnerved to rejoin the festivities so she made her way back to her room.

Who can I trust, she asked herself? *I'm just a kid. Why do they want to hurt me?*

Alice removed her fairy costume and handed it back to wardrobe. She told wardrobe what had happened.

"I'm so scared wardrobe, I'd like to crawl inside you and hide forever," she said.

"You're most welcome to Miss Alice but I don't think that you'd be very comfortable. You just need to get a good night's sleep dear. Things will look better in the morning," said wardrobe.

Alice curled up in bed and hid under the covers. She considered finding Sala'huddin and asking him to get her off the island, but could she trust him? She'd only known him one day. Tallbrick? He'd saved her; surely she could trust him not to hurt her. What about Herb and Miss Goddessbloom? Maybe it was Townie. Townie was the one who'd given her the glass of mead. She'd begun to feel queasy after drinking it.

When Trudy returned from the festival Alice pretended to be asleep. She couldn't face talking to anyone, not even Trudy.

Chapter Eleven

Alice tossed restlessly all night unable to sleep, in the morning she went down to breakfast on her own before Trudy woke up. She briefly looked around the school for her cousin, but had no idea how to find him or which house wing he was in. She eyed the skitters serving breakfast with suspicion, but hunger overcame fear and she helped herself to a cup of tea, some toast and a bowl of cereal, then sat at a table alone.

"Where's the entourage?" said a voice from behind her. It was Eloise, one of the queen genies. Alice was confused. "The fairy and the fat dwarf you hang around with; you three are usually joined at the hip. Or is that hips…?" Eloise mused and sat down next to Alice plonking her tray down on the table.

"Oh – you mean Trudy and Barton. She's a wood sprite and he's a goblin."

"Whatever!"

"Barton's on the mainland and Trudy is still asleep. I was hungry so I came on my own."

"Alice, are you okay sweetie? You look a little wrong." Eloise asked, showing concern.

"It's nothing. Do you know where Sala'huddin is?"

"Still asleep probably. We partied into the night. I'm only up cos I'm going to Zelda. I have got to get away to get some sunshine. The weather here is doing my head in."

"What's Zelda? Where is Zelda?" Alice asked.

"You don't know about Zelda!" Eloise laughed. "Oh! My! God! Sunshine! I'm talking wall to wall sunshine. Not like this cold, damp, windy, grey place. Zelda is an island off the coast of Costa Rica in the Pacific. It is warm. It is always warm. Hy Brasil and Zelda are like twins on opposite sides of the planet connected by a

91

wormhole and Hy Brasil is stuck at the cold end."

"What's a wormhole?" Alice asked curiously, imagining a tiny hole made by worms and momentarily forgetting her own problems.

"Look, I don't understand the physics, but it's like a tunnel that's a short cut between two places that are far away from each other. It takes a matter of seconds to get to Zelda once you step into the wormhole."

"Can I come?" Alice asked.

"I'd love to take you kid, but we'd have to get permission, I don't want to be accused of kidnapping."

"Zephyr tried to kill me last night!" Alice blurted out.

"What? When? How? OH! MY! GODDESS! Your cousin said there might be trouble. That's why your aunts sent him back. When did it happen?"

"Last night at the festival. Somebody drugged me – with something called wingot root - and Zephyr tried to suck me into a tree," Alice said. "That is a sentence I never thought I'd hear myself saying. Eloise I don't know who to trust. I'm so scared."

"How did you get away?"

"Master Tallbrick pulled me out," Alice replied. Eloise nodded thoughtfully.

"Yeah he's a bit of an old square, but he's pretty straight. Sounds like he's on your side. He'll have reported the attack already to the Goddess squad. Then, of course, there's us. You can always trust the djinn Alice.

Eat up – let's go and see Al!" Eloise said. Alice shoved the rest of her toast into her mouth and took a gulp of tea, then followed Eloise.

They headed for South house where all the djinn were boarded, and passed Trudy on the staircase as she was coming down for breakfast.

"Alice, why did you go for breakfast without me?"

Trudy asked.

"We're busy sprite!" Eloise snapped. "Alice doesn't have to explain herself to you."

Trudy looked hurt.

"I'll explain later," Alice whispered to Trudy as she raced to keep up with Eloise. Trudy watched Alice disappear into the South wing without her.

Eloise banged loudly on Sala'huddin's bedroom door. A few seconds later he opened the door wearing a blue satin bathrobe. His eyes were bloodshot from lack of rest.

"What do you want?" he mumbled looking at Eloise. He then noticed Alice behind her. "Hi cos, can you come back later I need another eight hours sleep?"

"No she can't!" Eloise said barging passed him into the room. "Zephyr tried to kill her last night."

"What? No way! I can't believe this. I only got here yesterday."

"Yes way! Maybe, he struck last night cos you came to protect her."

"Because of me? We have to get her out of here. Today! If anything happens to her my mum will kill me," he replied, now instantly focused.

"My thoughts exactly. Somebody doped her. We don't know who but ..."

"Townie," Alice interrupted.

"Who?" Sala'huddin and Eloise asked together.

"Townie – one of the skitters. She gave me a drink that was already poured. Trudy had one too but hers was from the back of the tray," Alice replied thoughtfully. "But it can't have been Townie – she's my friend."

"Look, it might not have been her," Sala'huddin said softly, sensing her distress. "Tell me what happened."

"I was at the party. Townie came over and gave me

a glass of mead. My head went fuzzy – I thought I was going to faint. I went over to the trees, to get away from the bonfire because I was hot and dizzy and feeling a bit sick. I leant on one of the trees and it sucked me inside. Next thing I know, Tallbrick reached inside and pulled me out."

"Classic Zephyr! Obviously, he's found a way to get through the magic shield the warlocks put up."

"Or someone has let him in. I'm due to go to Zelda this morning," Eloise said. "What if I take the kid with me?"

"We'll all go. Get your stuff and we'll meet out the front in half an hour. Eloise, don't let her out of your sight and Alice – don't tell anyone. Not your room mate – NOBODY."

"Got it!" Eloise replied.

"Don't I get a say in any of this?" Alice asked.

"No!" they both replied.

**

Master Tallbrick, Herb, Rosebay Thistledown and Miss Goddessbloom met together in the school office.

"We knew Zephyr would make a move on Alice," said Tallbrick, "we just didn't know it would be this soon."

"The question is – what are we going to do about it?" said Miss Goddessbloom.

"Surely the question should be; how are we going to stop him?" said Tallbrick. "And how did he get through the firewall you warlocks set up Herb? Another thing I'd like to ask you Athena is – are you sure you want to destroy Zephyr? He is your brother!"

"My loyalty is to this school and the children here. Times have moved on. We can never go back to ruling the way we did five thousand years ago in the age of wonder, from our home on Mount Olympus," Athena replied wistfully, casting a sideways glance at Herb.

"That's good to hear," said Tallbrick. "The humans are an unruly bunch. I can't see them bowing down to you lot again."

"The humans will eventually go the way of the dinosaurs," said Rosebay thoughtfully. "For the sake of the planet I don't think that will be a bad thing."

"There are other worlds we could go to – to escape from Zephyr," said Tallbrick.

"I don't think we're quite there yet," Herb put in.

"No, but it's always good to have an escape plan," Tallbrick insisted. They all nodded in agreement.

**

Alice, Sala'huddin and Eloise met on the Bonneville Goodhouse front steps. Alice had quickly changed out of her school uniform into a pair of jeans and a green top that wardrobe had picked out for her. Wardrobe had tried to insist she wrap up warmly, but she'd only had time to throw a tooth brush into her back pack before Eloise whisked her down stairs. Four streaks of lightning shot through black storm clouds that were rolling in from the north, filling the sky.

"Someone is coming," Eloise said warily.

"Yes and they don't look friendly," said Sala'huddin. Alice looked to the sky. The dark clouds were now swirling around the school.

"Is it a hurricane?" Alice asked.

"No, worse!" he replied as he laid his flying carpet on the ground. "Come on Alice, you're with me." He pulled Alice onto the carpet in front of him.

"We can't fly in this," Eloise yelled as the wind whipped around them.

"Stay low," he shouted.

"What if we go straight up," Alice screamed. Sala'huddin looked up. A small patch of blue sky was still visible in the centre of the vortex that now encircled the school.

"She's right," he motioned to Eloise. "Let's get above the cloud." Sala'huddin held Alice tightly around the waist and they all rose vertically on their carpets. Alice glanced back at the school and saw Trudy, watching them from a third floor window, her face pressed up against the glass. Within moments they soared confidently into the air. Alice gasped. It was exhilarating, like a roller coaster or the waltzers at a fun fair, so different to her misguided attempt to fly with Trudy over Lightwold town. Above the clouds the sun was shining but it was really cold. Alice shivered with cold and excitement.

Four bolts of lightning struck the lawn in front of the school. As each one struck the ground a warrior, in full body armour, flashed into being.

**

From their high vantage point high up in the stratosphere, they could see the swirling cloud below them beginning to dissipate and the four warriors standing in front of the school.

"Who are they?" she tried to say but her voice came out as a whisper. "Al – I can't breathe properly."

Sala'huddin nodded to Eloise and they descended slightly, to about four thousand feet. . A pair of golden eagles, soaring on columns of rising air, circled around them.

Sala'huddin, Alice and Eloise set course towards the snow capped Mountains of the Moon, which divided the two kingdoms of Lightwold and Dhuridhin.

"Where are we going? Who were those weird role

playing geeks who appeared in the lightning? Was that Zephyr?" Alice asked.

"It's best not to talk while you're flying Alice," Sala'huddin answered. "You swallow less bugs if you keep your mouth shut." Alice nodded and watched the scenery unfold below them. Alice could see the full extent of the Immortal Forest that was behind the school and all the way to the Bottomless Lake, and the Mountains of the Moon. The mountains, which had previously looked small and insignificant in the distance, now loomed imposingly, blocking out the sun as they approached them. The base of the mountains was covered by trails of mist that gave them a purplish colour. They landed safely and smoothly, in front of a small wooden cabin, with vines and ivy growing over its thatched roof. Eloise and Sala'huddin rolled up their carpets. It took a few seconds for Alice's eyes to adjust to the shadow light of the mountain after the bright sunshine high in the sky. She shivered.

"The cabin is the terminal and the portal to Zelda is inside the cabin," said Eloise. Her beautiful blue-black hair was windswept and in disarray. She still looked lovely.

"What happened back there Al? Who were those people that appeared? Was that Zephyr?" Alice repeated.

"No, those were the Norse gods – Odin, Thor, Kvasir and I think the other one was Tyr. All the big players are in town," Sala'huddin replied.

"Are they after me too?"

"I don't think so but they're all worried about Zephyr getting your power. Don't worry Alice you'll be safe once we get you to Zelda," he replied.

"Lighthorne Herb said I would be safe at the school," she said quietly.

"Well I wouldn't trust him as far as I could throw

him," Eloise put in. "I'm just scared they won't let Alice through the portal. We don't have any papers for her."

"The portal's permanently open – right?" Sala'huddin asked Eloise. She nodded. "Right – you distract the border guard – then as soon as he clears your papers – me and Alice will run through the gate and into the portal."

"Sounds like a plan!" Eloise replied. Alice looked confused.

"What border guard? What portal?" she asked.

They headed up the steps into the log cabin. Eloise led the way. Once inside Alice could not believe her eyes. She gasped. The inside of the log cabin was much bigger inside than it looked from outside. It was similar to an airport terminal with white marble floors, a glass ceiling, a row of check in desks that stretched into oblivion, and a gate, behind which was a blue undulating circle, about ten feet in diameter.

"That's the portal," Sala'huddin whispered to Alice. "Be ready to run." Alice nodded.

For all its size the terminal was manned by a single guard - a bored looking goblin, dressed in a maroon uniform. He reminded Alice of someone who worked in a fast food outlet. Eloise smiled at the man and looked at him seductively, fluttering her long, black eyelashes. Even though her hair was messy from the flight, she still looked beautiful. She dumped her bag in front of him and fished around inside pretending she couldn't find her papers. She giggled, and gazed into the guard's eyes hypnotically, mesmerising him.

"Now!" Sala'huddin yelled, grabbing Alice's arm and pulling her through the gate. The guard instantly turned and ran towards them.

"Stop!" he screamed. He was faster than he looked and he managed to grab hold of Alice's backpack.

Eloise leapfrogged over the check in desk and tripped the guard forcing him to release Alice as he fell.

"Ahhh!" he screamed.

Eloise grabbed her bag and skipped over the guard's prone body then followed Sala'huddin as he and Alice disappeared into the portal. Eloise turned and blew the guard a kiss.

A million beams of light and stars darted through Alice's eyes and out the back of her head. She prepared to scream but by the time her mouth opened she was thrown head over heels out onto a sandy beach and she was hit by a wall of heat. A sign before her read; 'WELCOME TO ZELDA' and beneath that were the words: 'HOME OF THE AMAZONIAN BEACH VOLLEY BALL TEAM'.

**

Alice had never seen the sea and sky so sapphire blue and sand that was so white. A row of palm trees and thirty giant heads lined the beach. Behind the heads was a row of white circular chalets with thatched roofs.

"This looks like heaven," she said as she stood up and dusted the sand from her clothes. Three female skitters, all wearing coconut brassieres and grass skirts, approached to welcome them. Alice, Sala'huddin and Eloise were each offered a lei, a garland of flowers and were led to an arrivals desk on the beach. It was quite different to the departure terminal in Lightwold. This was a simple structure with a bamboo pole in each of its four corners and a roof thatched with coconut grass. An officious looking male skitter sat behind a wooden desk. He wore a grass skirt with a burgundy jacket that was a little too small for him.

"The child is not cleared for transport," he said as they approached the desk.

"But she's already here," said Eloise. The guard looked confused.

"She's my cousin. I have the right to bring her here," said Sala'huddin.

The border guard looked at Alice.

"Is that true?" he asked. Alice nodded. The guard shrugged, "Very well, I suppose it will be alright. Here are the keys to three beach front chalets. The buffet is open 24 hours a day. Have a nice vacation."

He handed them three wooden keys and pointed them in the direction of the row of white, straw roofed chalets further up the beach.

"This is excellent!" Alice exclaimed as she skipped ahead. "It is so warm! I'm starving can we go and eat?"

When they found their allotted chalets, Sala'huddin gave Alice the key to centre hut.

"Get settled in Alice, then we'll go for something to eat."

Alice opened the door and looked around her chalet. It was a simple circular room with a window that faced the blue ocean. The floor was sandy, covered with a mat made of rushes. The chalet contained a bathroom with shower, bed and a wicker clothes hamper.

"Good morning," said the clothes hamper when Alice entered the chalet.

"Oh wow! Are you like the magic wardrobe at school?"

"Yes, however, I only stock summer wear. Can I recommend an outfit for you to wear to breakfast?"

"Is it still breakfast time here?"

"I believe, due to time zones, we are about five or six hours behind Hy Brasil. Now can I recommend shorts and a T shirt with jelly bean sandals? It gets rather warm here later in the day."

Alice picked out an outfit and changed out of the clothes she'd travelled in.

"I wish my friend Trudy was here," she said.

"Maybe you could arrange for a message to be sent to her through the portal," hamper said.

"No, my cousin doesn't want anyone to know I'm here. We're hiding because I'm in danger. Trudy is my best friend and I couldn't even say goodbye."

**

"Invite them to join us in the Inner Sanctum," Athena Goddessbloom snarled to her waiting skitter, Dorocha, as she watched Odin, Thor, Kvasir and Tyr, the Norse gods, striding across the lawn in front of Bonneville Goodhouse. She nodded to Tallbrick, Rosebay and Herb. "Let's retire to the Sanctum. The office is rather small for entertaining such large guests." They followed her to an adjoining room.

The Sanctum had a north facing window and a boardroom table in the middle, big enough to seat sixteen people. The walls were lined with bookcases. They each took seats at the far end of the table while they waited for the Norse to join them. Odin entered first, dramatically throwing open both doors, to emphasise his presence. Athena and Lighthorne Herb stood as a mark of respect.

"Athena!" Odin boomed as they entered. "You got old."

"Thank you Odin," she acknowledged. "Please, take a seat."

"We do not need to sit!"

"I find conversations tend to go better when all participants are sitting comfortably," said Athena.

"You!" Odin yelled at Dorocha who had accompanied them. "Bring ale! Four flagons!" Dorocha nodded obediently and ran away.

"They don't conform to stereotype at all, do they?"

Rosebay whispered sarcastically.

"It's a little early in the day for alcohol isn't it?" Herb stated.

"It was a long flight," Odin replied. He motioned to Thor, Kvasir and Tyr. "Sit!" They all stood seven feet tall and as they moved to sit, the chairs around the boardroom table seemed ridiculously small. They perched on the chairs uncomfortably. Dorocha quickly returned with four large flagons and placed them in front of the Vikings.

"Now! To what do we owe the pleasure of this unannounced visit?" Athena asked.

"I think you know," Odin replied. "There has been a resurgence in the force. The runes are forecasting a change of power and we are concerned. Zephyr is on the move."

"Perhaps you should take less notice of your withered rune casters. No one knows what Zephyr's plans are, or, what the impact would be should he ever attain the power he covets," Rosebay interjected.

"I think it is fairly obvious," said Kvasir. "We no longer hold power over the humans in this world, though their reign will be short lived. We should never have shown them how to use electricity. Zephyr will try to control us in the magical world, should he get what he wants. Speaking of whom – where is the girl?"

"We don't need to involve her," said Herb.

"I want to meet this girl whose very existence is the cause of so much trouble to us all," Odin insisted. He pointed to Dorocha who was hovering in the background. "You! Fetch Alice Devises! Now!" Dorocha nodded and retreated from the room.

"The girl is innocent!" Herb said. "She is just a pawn in a very nasty game."

"We were wondering if there are any ulterior motives here," said Tyr. "Maybe you wish to use the girl's powers for your own means."

"I resent that insinuation!" Athena snapped.

"Why? You Greek gods are known for stabbing each other in the back. Maybe you're trying to get one up on your brother," said Tyr. A tiny knock came at the door.

"Come in!" Athena called angrily. Dorocha entered sheepishly. "Speak!" Athena yelled.

"I'm so sorry," he whispered. "She's gone."

"Gone!" Odin roared, rising to his feet. His chair crashed to the floor. Dorocha cowered and began to cry. "What do you mean she's gone?"

"I went to her room, and her room mate said Miss Alice flew off with her cousin just before you got here," he whimpered.

"Flew off? This is ridiculous!" said Thor. "You're supposed to be keeping her safe."

"She's not a prisoner. They've probably just gone out for the day," said Rosebay in an attempt to calm the situation. A knock came at the door and a second skitter, Juan, entered the room.

"Excuse me Mistress Goddessbloom. I am sorry to interrupt but there has been an unauthorised transportation involving three of our students at the portal terminal. They assaulted the border guard and fled through the portal," he announced. Athena shook her head and sighed deeply.

"Do we know which students are involved?" she asked through gritted teeth.

"The border guard believes they were three genies," Juan replied, "because they flew in on magic carpets. There were two teenagers and a child."

"Get out!" Athena said to the two skitters. The Norse glared at the others accusingly.

"It seems as if you have no control over your students. Find the girl!" Odin ordered, banging his ale flagon down onto the table, and spilling the contents. He signalled to his comrades to leave. They rose abruptly and left the Sanctum slamming the doors behind them. Once outside on the lawn they disappeared in four flashes of lightning.

"I hate those guys!" said Tallbrick. "Have you seen how big they are? They're at least three feet taller than me!"

When the Norse had departed Athena turned to the others.

"Back to business," she said. "We still need to discover what happened last night and who was involved.

Herb, it seems as if Sala'huddin has taken Alice to Zelda. I knew he'd be trouble. I should never have let him return to the school. You need to go to Zelda and get her back before all out war breaks out." Herb nodded in agreement.

"Alice told me that the skitter, Townie Thorne, served her mead just before she began to feel unwell," said Tallbrick.

"I'll interrogate Townie," said Athena. "I expect the warlocks will be getting involved soon."

"I'll keep them in check for now but we'd better move fast," said Herb.

**

"So what's the plan?" Alice asked Sala'huddin as she sipped on a fruit cocktail which contained more fruits than she knew the name of.

"I don't know," he mused. "I'm kind of making it up as I go along."

"I'm going to catch some rays," Eloise said. She picked up a blue beach towel and slinked towards the beach.

"Thank you," Alice said quietly.

"For what?" he asked with a mouth full of coconut.

"For helping me and risking getting into trouble."

"It's my job. You're family – and I enjoy getting into trouble. Besides what can they do to me?"

"Take away your powers and lock you up."

"Once we're out of the magic shields I can just blink and go anywhere in the world. You'll be able to do that soon too. Put your hand on the Ruksana stone and you can go anywhere in the universe."

"What's a Ruksana stone?"

"A big granite thingy my mum looks after, and that's got loads of writing like hieroglyphs and can phase shift you anywhere."

Alice finished her second breakfast of the day, and she and Sala'huddin joined Eloise on the beach.

"Exactly how hot does it get here?" Alice asked as she lay back on a sun bed next to Eloise.

"I don't know – 30 – maybe 40 degrees. What scale do you want it in?" Eloise replied.

"You could have just said – really hot! Can I go and play in the sea?"

"Don't go too far in. There are sharks and monsters and things in there that will eat you," Sala'huddin said. "I don't want to be blamed if you get eaten." Alice got up from her sun bed and ran to the sea shore.

"Babysitting is really frustrating," Eloise said once Alice was out of earshot.

"She's family. It has to be done."

Alice paddled up to her knees while Eloise and Sala'huddin sunbathed. She picked up some colourful shells to give to Trudy as a present if she ever went back to school. When the pockets of her shorts were bulging she walked back up the beach to Eloise and Sala'huddin.

"I'm bored and it's too hot," she said. "And I'm

going really brown but I think my arms might be getting sunburnt."

"If you're bored, go and get us all ice creams from the buffet," Sala'huddin replied. "And while you're there ask the skitters for some sun cream."

"Okay," she said and skipped up the beach.

"I really didn't think this through," he said. "I can't look after a kid."

"Hey we didn't have time to think. Remember Zephyr tried to kidnap her last night?" Eloise replied.

"That seems like a long time ago," he said as he lay back on his sun bed. "I hate that school. Let's never go back."

"Sounds like a plan."

Alice returned awkwardly carrying a tray containing three huge, multi-coloured ice cream floats, and with her nose, arms and legs covered in green sun block.

"The skitters should have carried that for you," Eloise said, helping herself to one of the floats.

"I told them I could do it," Alice replied. She passed an ice cream to Sala'huddin and sat on the sand next to him.

"They're servants. They are here to serve us," Eloise said. "You should have made one of them carry the tray."

"I didn't mind," Alice protested. "I'm not used to having people do stuff for me."

At that moment the portal glowed, showing there was an incoming traveller and they watched as Lighthorne Herb stepped through. He was dressed in his usual all black outfit and looked totally out of place on the beach. One of the tiny skitters tried to give him a welcoming flower garland but he dismissed her. He ignored the clerk at the arrival's desk and marched straight towards them.

"Uh oh! Here comes trouble," Alice said as she tried

to hide behind her cousin.

"I know!" he replied but Sala'huddin was not referring to Herb. He was staring across the sea to black storm clouds that were gathering on the horizon.

"What's that? Is it the Norse men or Zephyr?" Alice asked.

"Worse!" he replied. "It's my mum!"

**

Herb strode across the beach towards them.

"You!" he said pointing to Eloise and Sala'huddin. "You are in more trouble than you can imagine!" They both rose to stand and Alice hid behind Sala'huddin. Eloise covered herself with the beach towel she'd been lying on.

"Hey man – how you doing?" Sala'huddin asked guiltily.

"Don't you dare 'Hey man' me! You attacked a border guard, kidnapped a child and transported her through the portal illegally."

"We were trying to save her life!" Eloise protested.

"How can I have kidnapped her? She's my cousin," said Sala'huddin.

"That's right! They didn't kidnap me," Alice put in. "And – what the Hell – you never told me I had a family! It's the first thing you should have told me! You know, that morning when you came for me and we were sitting in McDonalds – not let me find out, by accident, months later. I've been at the bloomin' school for months Herb and you never told me – I HAVE A FAMILY!"

"Be quiet Alice!" Herb snapped. The beating sun was already turning his nose red. Alice glanced out to sea. The storm clouds were quickly approaching the island and in the distance Alice could see her aunt

107

surfing on top of the clouds, riding high on a flying carpet. She rode the carpet standing, and looked magnificent with her long black, plaited hair and turquoise scarf flowing behind her.

"I think you'd better discuss this with my mum," Sala'huddin said.

"Alice, get your belongings!" Herb ordered.

"I will not! I want to wait for my aunty," Alice replied stubbornly. "The aunty YOU never told me about!"

The clouds dissipated and Noorjahan glided gently to the beach next to her son. She stepped off the carpet and a skitter ran to present her with a flower garland which she bent down to graciously accept. She wore an elegant, turquoise salwar kameez decorated with diamonds and silver sequins and looked stunning, without a hair out of place.

"Mum!" Sala'huddin shouted as he moved to embrace her but Noorjahan pushed him to one side.

"Aliyah, my Aliyah," she cried as she grabbed hold of Alice. "We've missed you so much. We never stopped searching for you my darling." She smothered Alice's face with kisses. Alice pulled back awkwardly.

"Much as I hate to interrupt this touching family reunion I have to return Alice to Bonneville Goodhouse immediately," said Herb.

"Herby! Darling," exclaimed Noorjahan as she gracefully turned to Herb. "Why, you look as dashingly handsome as always. It is so lovely here, and I've only just arrived. I insist you let me have more time with Aliyah."

"My shoes are full of sand and it's ridiculously hot. I am taking her back now," he snapped and grabbed Alice's arm.

"No you are not!" Alice said pulling away from him.

"Let's all go up to the buffet. I've had a long flight

and I'm so thirsty," said Noorjahan. "I need to get out of the sun too." Herb sighed and grudgingly conceded.

"Very well. Ten minutes. You can come back to the school with us you know."

"Me and Eloise will stay here," said Sala'huddin.

"Yes, I'll speak to you later," his mother replied sternly.

Herb, Alice and Noorjahan sat together at a table in the buffet. They ordered pineapple cocktails.

"I can't tell you how happy we were when we finally found you my darling, Aliyah," said Noorjahan.

"Why didn't you come and get me straight away? Why did it take you all those years to find me? And why do you keep calling me Aliyah?"

"Aliyah is your real name darling."

"Her name is Alice, the name given to her by her father's family," Herb interjected.

"Let's just say that Alice is your northern European name, but Aliyah is your real name given to you by your mother."

"I like it," she said thoughtfully, "but I'll stick with Alice."

"Very well. When your mother…. During the fight, when she tried to send you to us – things were crazy. You could have ended up anywhere in the universe. We didn't know where to look."

"I was in England."

"We know that now but until your powers manifested we had no way to track you." She took Alice's hand. "And now we've found you. I wanted to come and get you immediately but the warlocks got all huffy and demanded you be placed in neutral territory."

"The school?"

"Yes, however, I believe you should now return with me. I was in Hawaii. It's beautiful there and my gentleman friend is Kanu – he's one of the Hawaiian gods. You will love it," Noorjahan stated adamantly.

"That's not going to happen," Herb replied.

"How did you know I was in Zelda?" Alice asked them both.

"I can always sense where Sala'huddin is, he's my son, and he would never have dared leave Hy Brasil without you. I sent him back to the school to take care of you."

Herb shuffled uncomfortably in his chair. Sweat was forming on his forehead.

"I think it's about time we returned to the school," he said.

"I don't want to go back," Alice said firmly. She proceeded to tell her aunt the events that led to her fleeing to Zelda.

"Well!" said Noorjahan. "It's obvious she's not safe at the school anymore. I was prepared to give my son a good telling off but it seems as if he did the right thing."

"He did not do the right thing. They attacked a border guard."

"Is he hurt?"

"No, but that is not the point. They travelled through the portal without permission." Noorjahan flicked her hair.

"Oh poof! So what! Paperwork! What are we – mortals? Drink your juice Herb; she's coming to Hawaii with me! And though Sala'huddin's attempts to keep Aliyah safe were amateurish, he meant well. So I insist he not get into any trouble."

"The Norse are threatening war if we don't bring her back," Herb exaggerated, the sweat on his forehead began to run down his face. Noorjahan sighed. Alice shuffled her feet, she was getting bored.

"I want to go to Hawaii," she said. They ignored her.

"She is my dead sister's only child," Noorjahan

pleaded softly. "Please Herby darling, she should be with her family."

"I understand, but all the factions fear her power, should she join any particular one. The school is safe. We're interrogating the skitters to find out if any of them are involved with Zephyr and we're putting up extra firewalls as a precaution. I doubt Zephyr is capable of a full blown attack on the school. There are too many of us."

Noorjahan looked at Alice thoughtfully.

"We don't want war do we Aliyah?" she said.

"But I want to come with you," Alice replied.

"If someone was hurt because of you – could you ever forgive yourself?"

"No," Alice sighed resentfully. "But I don't see why everybody is so crazy for me. Nobody ever wanted me before. I was passed from one place to another because they didn't want me, now everyone wants me. It's weird."

"You will be very powerful one day darling," said Noorjahan. "The warlocks and the Norse are fearful, and though I never want to let you out of my sight again, peace is always the best solution. Maybe you should return to the school."

"Good!" said Herb forcefully. "Let's go back now."

"No," said Noorjahan. "We can stay here – in paradise – at least for one night! I want to get to know my niece."

"I don't believe this," Herb gasped. "It's too hot!"

"Oh come on Herby darling, stop moaning," Noorjahan said with a smile. "It's party night – every night here on Zelda. Change out of those stuffy clothes; I know you'll look amazing in a Hawaiian shirt and shorts. Let's have some fun!"

Chapter Twelve

The next day Alice returned through the portal with a disgruntled Herb. His nose was burnt and he had not enjoyed the party night. Noorjahan had tried to get him to fire walk and dance with the skitters which he'd ungraciously declined to do. Alice fell asleep early in a deck chair and Eloise and Sala'huddin had crept away from the crowd to watch the stars alone on the beach.

Due to the time difference it was late afternoon when they arrived back at the school. Athena Goddessbloom met them at the door.

"Alice," she said warmly. "Welcome back! You've had an eventful couple of days. I want you to know that we intend to keep you safe from now on."

"My cousin's not going to get into trouble is he?" Alice asked.

"Though he had good intentions, he did break some very strict rules..." Miss Goddessbloom began to say but Herb gave her a stern sideways glance. Alice looked at her angrily. "But," Athena continued, "he won't be punished too harshly."

**

"Trudy," Alice called as she entered her dorm room. Trudy came out of the bathroom.

"Where have you been?" said Trudy excitedly. "You just flew off and everyone was looking for you. There was this huge storm and these Vikings appeared in flashes of lightning."

"I'll tell you everything but look what I got for you," said Alice. She gave Trudy the shells she'd collected on the beach, the flower garland the Zelda skitters had given her and a shell necklace Noorjahan had bought for her. She also gave Trudy the paper umbrellas that she'd collected from the cocktails and ice creams she'd eaten. "We went to Zelda, which is a magic island like this one, but really hot, because Zephyr tried to kill me. Then my aunty, she's really pretty, and Herb both came for me. She wanted me to go to Hawaii cos she's got this boyfriend there, but Herb wants me here so I can stop a war!" The girls burst out laughing and hugged. "Zelda was really nice but sooo boring and sooo hot. Herb got sunburnt and the skitters plastered me with green sun block. It would have been okay if you'd been there and Barton of course, but there was nothing to do except drink fancy fruity drinks and eat ice cream. There was a cool party last night. Is Barton back yet?"

"He's back tomorrow. I really missed you. I wish I could have gone with you."

"Sorry, everything happened really fast, it was like – here comes a storm, let's fly! Then Sala'huddin beat up the border guard," Alice exaggerated without taking a breath. "He's so strong and really good looking. I think him and Eloise have a thing. And whoosh! We went through this portal which was blue but with these mad lights, and we ended up on a beach on the other side of the world."

"What's the portal travel like?"

"It's like jumping into a puddle that's not wet and the lights go through your head but don't hurt you, and zoom, you're there. Mad and really cool." They laughed and the problems of the last days disappeared. "Have I told you how hot it was?"

**

The term resumed and life returned to as normal as it could be for a magic school. Alice was disturbed by

Townie's absence but whenever she asked, no one, including the other skitters, would tell her where Townie was. She constantly felt as if she was being watched but assumed it was the extra security Herb had promised Noorjahan. Sala'huddin checked in on her daily. The days grew short and a cold wind blew endlessly off the Atlantic. Sometimes Alice wished she could go back to Zelda just to feel warm again.

A few weeks later that term, Alice joined her fellow djinn in the Elemental Physics lab. She loved this class – all the students were friendly, Farzeena was her favourite teacher, and it was the one class she shared with Sala'huddin. She made herself comfortable at the front of the class in her usual place, on a cushion between Sheharazade and Sherzeen, while Sala'huddin sat at the back of the room with the older boys and girls.

Farzeena stood at the front of the class. Beside her was a tall object, covered by a teal coloured satin cloth.

"Today," Farzeena said. "I have a treat for the younger members of the class." A murmur of excitement spread around the room. Farzeena dramatically removed the satin cloth, like an amateur magician pulling a table cloth from beneath a pile of crockery, to reveal a huge bamboo birdcage containing a large bird. The three youngest classmates looked intrigued. The bird's turquoise, emerald and purple feathers were iridescent, and she shimmered and appeared to change colour whenever she moved.

"This is Comet," Farzeena announced. "She is a Feather Glow or Impundulu – otherwise known as a lightning bird. In certain tribes in Africa the fat of an Impundulu is extracted by cooking the birds, and used in magic spells. It is supposed to be the fuel that sets on fire whenever the Impundulu throws lightning bolts." Comet shrieked! "You know I would never do that to you Comet."

"I should think not!" Comet replied. Farzeena continued.

"The fat and the eggs of the Impundulu are also used in tribal medicine and by African witch doctors for spells."

"Is it a parrot?" Alice enquired.

"I most certainly am not," Comet answered snappily. "Parrots are mindless creatures. I am sentient."

"Then why are you in a cage?" Alice asked cheekily. The class sniggered.

"For your safety and my convenience," Farzeena said giving the younger children a fierce look, hoping they'd shut up and not upset Comet. They all got the hint. "Comet has a gift for you new students; come forward please."

Alice, Sherzeen and Sheharazade stepped forward to the cage. Farzeena opened the door and Comet hopped out on top of the bamboo cage.

"You're very beautiful," said Sherzeen.

"You should see me under a UV light – my feathers glow," Comet replied.

"Farzeena – please," Comet said. Farzeena passed a silken bundle to each of the younger children. "Open them please," Comet commanded. They all obediently undid the ribbons on their parcels. Inside each was an individual Faberge style egg. Alice gasped. Her egg was lilac and encrusted with tiny diamonds and sapphires but it weighed less than a feather. She glanced over at her classmates whose eggs were equally stunning. Sheharazade's egg was deep purple covered in a golden lattice, and Sherzeen's egg was pale blue and studded with garnets.

"You are all very powerful creatures," Comet said. "But there may be times when you need a little power boost. These eggs are my gift to you as a thank you to the djinn for their eternal protection of my species from

African witch doctors. Keep them close to you at all times." Comet bowed his head reverently.

"Take very good care of these eggs," said Farzeena looking directly at Alice. "It may come to pass that one day you will need their help."

**

"Did you ever get an egg?" Alice asked Sala'huddin as they walked from class.

"I most certainly did," he replied.

"Where do you keep it for safety?" she asked.

"That," he said with a wink, "is for me to know, and is for you to mind your own business."

Alice placed her Impundulu egg on her bedside table over night and in the day time, carried it with her wherever she went.

**

Every Wednesday, first period of the day was History of Magic with Master Tallbrick. Alice prepared for a snooze fest. As nice a guy as he was; his style of teaching sent Alice into daydreams. Each minute dragged and Alice found herself staring out of the window hoping that something – anything – would happen.

"Miss Devises – see me at the end of the lesson please," Tallbrick snapped when he noticed Alice's concentration wandering.

Oh God, no, she thought, *I'm in trouble again!*

An hour later, Alice stood at Tallbrick's desk as all the other students filed out of the classroom.

"Alice," Tallbrick said with a smile. She'd been expecting a telling off and was rather taken aback. "Don't look so worried. I don't bite. I just wanted to talk to you about doing some extra curricular activities."

"Does that mean more work?" she sighed, envisioning hours of homework, pouring over Tallbrick's boring text books.

"I think you need to be more prepared, should there be another attack on your life."

"And how will more reading prepare me?"

"What I was proposing Alice was learning more practical magic Alice," he said. Her face lit up.

"Yeah – that would be great. Can you teach me? When? Where? I'll be there."

"Meet me tonight in the gym at 7pm."

"Can I bring my mates?" she asked cheekily.

"Not too many. I want to keep this on the QT."

"I don't know what that means but I'll be there."

"Good! Wear suitable attire."

**

That evening after dinner, Alice, with Trudy and Barton in tow, headed for the gymnasium. It was dark outside and all the gym lights were fully blazing. Tallbrick was already inside, practising what appeared to be a form of Tai Chi. He was wearing a jogging suit and trainers which, Alice thought, made him look even shorter than usual.

"Alice – good – you're on time," Tallbrick said. Trudy and Barton found a seat in the stands and Barton produced a bag of popcorn for them to munch on while they watched Alice's lesson.

"Right! Let us begin. Have you brought your Impundulu egg with you?" Tallbrick asked. Alice nodded and produced it from her pocket. She held it out to him. "Never, never, never give that egg to anyone Alice. Not to me, or to any other teacher at this school.

Do you understand? It is very important." Alice nodded. "Right, has anyone explained how to use this egg?" She shook her head. He continued: "Hold the egg aloft," he ordered. She looked confused. "Up in the air," he sighed. Alice did what she was told. "Hold it tightly in your fist or you might drop it. Now I need you to concentrate. Can you feel the eggs power flowing through you?"

"Not really," she replied. Nothing happened.

"Concentrate harder – close your eyes if you need to. Can you feel it now?"

"Maybe," she lied. She closed her eyes tightly and tried to focus on the egg.

"Concentrate – concentrate…"

"I am bloomin' concentrating," she snapped.

"Alice, open your eyes," Tallbrick said with a smile. Alice did as Tallbrick said and as she did so she saw, to her amazement, a blue beam, emanating from the egg, forming a square perimeter around the gymnasium floor. Trudy and Barton whooped and hollered.

"That's amazing Alice. Well done!" they cheered.

"That, Alice, is the beginning of what the egg can do. Today, I want you to see how long you can hold the energy perimeter. And envision anything else you may be able to get it to do." Tallbrick joined Trudy and Barton in the stands and helped himself to their popcorn while Alice stayed on the gym floor to perfect her skill. Within minutes Alice managed to transfigure the blue beams into animal shapes, darts, a Christmas tree and waves.

"This is so cool," she squealed excitedly as blue stars danced across the high gymnasium ceiling. "I have the power!" she exclaimed.

"That's enough for today," Tallbrick announced after about forty minutes. "We don't want to drain the egg."

"Ohhh!" Alice, Trudy and Barton all moaned, together.

"Next week," said Tallbrick as they walked from the gym, "I will show you how to use the egg to form a protective shield."

They met in the gym each Wednesday evening over the next few weeks. Tallbrick introduced Alice to both magic and marital arts. Alice learned that with concentration, the blue energy from the Impundulu egg could form a circular shield that withstood anything Tallbrick hit it with. It always surprised her how spry Tallbrick actually was. When Tallbrick and Alice practised various martial arts attack and defence moves, Trudy and Barton aped whatever moves Tallbrick taught Alice and sparred with each other, whilst watching from the sidelines. The one thing Alice struggled with were time freezes. No matter how hard she tried – nothing would freeze for her.

"What am I doing wrong," she asked Tallbrick repeatedly. He just laughed.

"You can't be good at everything Alice. You're improving in every other department, so just be grateful.

"How come a short guy like you is so strong?" Alice asked cheekily one evening as they parried with wooden staves.

"Did you ever see Master Yoda in the Star Wars movies?" he replied.

"Was he the small, green dude who does adverts on the telly?" she replied. Tallbrick sighed with exasperation.

"He was a Jedi master …. The point I am trying to make Alice is that size is irrelevant. It is technique, focus and power that are important."

"But Yogi wasn't real was he? It was just a film," said Alice as she knocked Tallbrick to the floor and proudly stood over him with her right foot on his chest.

"His name was Yoda, but never mind Alice – well fought."

**

Alice loved the sessions with Tallbrick and with his training and the support of her friends she grew confident in her own abilities. She began to carry the Impundulu egg on a chain around her neck. Sometimes, before sports lessons – Barton, Trudy and Alice practised the martial arts moves Tallbrick had showed them. However, in mid December, Miss Goddessbloom called Alice to her office.

"It has been brought to my attention," Miss Goddessbloom said as Alice stood before her, "that you have being receiving extra tuition from Master Tallbrick."

"Yes," Alice confirmed, "he's been helping me practice my magic skills."

"Master Tallbrick is a history teacher. He cannot be seen to be showing favouritism towards any particular student. I cannot allow these sessions to continue."

"But…"

"What if you were injured during these lessons? Master Tallbrick would be held responsible. Therefore on the grounds of health and safety I absolutely forbid any more of these training sessions and they will cease immediately."

"But…" Alice protested.

"There is nothing more to be said Miss Devices. Master Tallbrick has been informed of my decision. Now get back to your studies. I want no more of this nonsense."

Alice was angry and frustrated and stormed out of the office, slamming the door behind her. She could tell by Miss Goddessbloom's tone of voice that she was not going to be swayed but Alice was burning with resentment.

After the next History of Magic lesson Alice tried to talk to Tallbrick.

"Master Tallbrick – maybe we could practise in secret," she begged. "I promise I won't tell anyone." But Tallbrick shook his head.

"I'm sorry Alice, but they've put me on academic probation."

"Why? I don't understand what we did wrong."

"Neither do I, really. Some clap trap about health and safety. But Goddessbloom was adamant that I can only teach you history and only in a classroom."

"This is stupid and not fair," she said. "I don't care about the health and safety police." Tallbrick nodded in agreement. They both new the consequences of defying Miss Goddessbloom and there was nothing further they could do.

**

One evening, a few days before the end of term, as Alice and Trudy were doing their homework in their dorm room; a note, sealed in a white envelope, was pushed under the study door. It was addressed to Alice. She opened the letter cautiously. It read:

Dear Alice

I know your parents are still alive and being held prisoner by Zephyr. There is a way you and I can rescue them together. Come to my study tonight at 8pm. COME ALONE AND TELL NO ONE!

TALLBRICK

Alice read the note twice.

"What does it say?" asked Trudy excitedly. Alice thought carefully. She wasn't supposed to say what was in the note, but Trudy was her best friend.

"It's from Tallbrick," she confided. "It says he thinks my parents are still alive and he knows a way to rescue them."

"It's a strange way to tell you something so important. I know your sparring sessions have been nixed but why didn't he just tell you in class? Maybe it's a trap!"

"But maybe he needs to meet me in secret because he doesn't know who to trust and doesn't want Miss Goddessbloom to find out," Alice said thoughtfully.

"I know he was training you, but do you know if you can trust him completely?"

"I think so. He saved me Trudy. He pulled me out of that tree at the All Hallows Eve festival, and he's taught me more than any other teacher here."

"That is true – what about your cousin? Should we tell him?"

"No, not yet. Let's go and see what Tallbrick has to say before I involve Sala'huddin."

"Okay but I'll come with you," Trudy insisted.

"The note says to come alone."

"Me and Barton will wait outside his office, just to make sure it's safe."

Chapter Thirteen

At 7.55pm Alice slipped her Impundulu egg around her neck and put her mobile phone in her pocket. There was still no signal but she always kept it charged and felt better carrying it with her. She, Trudy and Barton made their way to Tallbrick's study. They could hear music coming from the room, so Alice knocked loudly on the door. There was no reply.

"What shall I do?" Alice asked.

"Go in!" said Barton. "He told you to come."

"That's true; he did." Alice turned the door knob and pushed the study door open. Barton and Trudy dutifully stayed behind in the corridor.

"Master Tallbrick!" she called loudly as she entered the study. "It's me – Alice."

The music was really loud in the study and there was no sign of Tallbrick, but a fire was blazing in the fire place making the room stuffy and uncomfortably hot. It was the first time Alice had been in Tallbrick's study but she noticed it was similar to Herb's and Miss Goddessbloom's in that there was a desk, several lamps, a studded leather chair, a leather couch, and bookshelves stuffed with ancient tomes. The music was coming from a red box containing a black disc that was spinning around and around. When the tune stopped a grey arm lifted up and returned to the outside edge of the disc, starting the music again.

She found a note on the desk next to the music box, which read;

ALICE – *PUSH THE BUTTON*

"Which button?" she asked herself. "This is stupid!" She returned to door and invited Barton and Trudy in. Barton crossed to the music box.

"What is this?" he asked. The girls shook their

heads. "Maybe it's like a CD player." He lifted the arm off the black disc and removed the disc from the box.

"It says Wonderful, Wonderful by someone called Johnny Mathis," he read.

"It was very loud," said Trudy.

"I liked it," said Alice. "Anyway, this note here in spider writing says 'Push the button'. Which button do you think it means?"

"And where is Tallbrick?" Barton asked as he returned the black disc to the box. They looked around the study pushing every button they could find but nothing happened. Barton sat down on the couch. He checked the time – it was 8.15pm.

"Maybe we should give up," Trudy said.

"No I have to find Tallbrick. He thinks my parents are alive and may know a way to rescue them."

"Maybe we should go and get your cousin. He's big and knows a lot more magic than we do," said Barton.

"Is this a button?" Trudy asked, spotting a lever on the bookcase.

"It looks more like a handle," said Barton rising from the couch. "Push it anyway." Alice pushed the lever while Trudy and Barton looked on. The bookcase swung open revealing an unlit spiral, stone staircase.

"Maybe he's down there," said Trudy.

"Maybe I should go down on my own," said Alice apprehensively.

"I don't think you should, I can freeze time if there's any trouble. You haven't quite mastered that yet," said Trudy.

"Yeah, and I can run around and get in people's way!" Baron put in.

"Oh thank God! I really didn't want to go down on my own," said Alice with a sigh of relief.

Tentatively, they crept down the poorly lit stairwell in single file. Alice went first using her mobile phone as a torch. Trudy and Barton followed cautiously behind her. There was a very dim light coming from the study above. The stairs were uneven, narrow on one side, but wider towards the edge, and the staircase seemed to go on forever.

"Has anyone been counting these steps?" Alice shouted to Trudy and Barton after a few minutes.

"No, but it seems like we've come down hundreds already," said Trudy.

"I just hope we find a lift at the bottom I don't fancy climbing all the way back up," said Barton.

"Wait a minute," said Alice, "I think there's a room here." The staircase continued on downwards but they decided to investigate the murky room. Barton felt around the walls and found a light switch.

"Shield your eyes," he announced.

"Why? Ow!" said Alice as Barton flicked a switch and light filled the room.

"Oh my God! It's identical to Tallbrick's study," Trudy said. "Wait! Did we not just climb down like a million steps?"

"Yeah, course we did," Barton replied.

"Then where's the stairwell gone?"

A bookcase was in the place the stairwell should have been, fixed firmly to the wall, with no lever or handle to be pushed.

"This is crazy. Are we imagining stuff?"

"There's no music box in this study. Maybe we've been poisoned like when Zephyr tried to kidnap you and we're imagining weird stuff," said Barton as he turned the leather office chair around to sit down.

"Aaargh!" they all screamed in unison as Barton sat down on the lap of a crystallised Tallbrick.

"Ew! Ew! Ew!" Barton screamed as he jumped up and ran to hide behind the girls. "Gross! Gross! Gross!"

"What the Hell happened to him?" Alice yelled.

"He's dead! He's dead!" cried Barton.

"No, look at that brown sticky stuff he's covered in. That's amber. Tree sap that crystallises," said Trudy. "I think he's been preserved."

"What's this?" Alice asked crossing to a large, grey metallic box in the corner of the room that none of them had previously noticed. "It looks like a freezer."

"There wasn't a freezer in Tallbrick's study," said Trudy. "I mean – the study we came from." Alice opened the freezer door.

"Aaargh!" They all screamed again as Townie's frozen body fell out and landed, face down, on the floor.

"Let's go! We have to tell someone," said Alice as they all ran for the study door and out, into the corridor beyond. They began running towards where the main hallway and school offices should have been, but no matter how fast and how far they ran the corridor still stretched out before them.

"What's happening?" Barton puffed. They stopped running. The corridor now stretched endlessly in both directions.

"I don't think we're in the school any more," Alice stated. "This is magical. A spell or something. There's no point in going down the corridor. We're going to have to search in each of these rooms and every one of these doors to see what's behind them, and if there's a way out. By the way – thanks again for coming with me – I could have been here on my own. I just wish we'd taken your advice Barton and brought Sala'huddin with us."

At that moment, in the distance, a pin prick blue light appeared at one end of the corridor. It was moving towards them at speed and getting bigger.

"What the….." Barton said as the light whizzed passed his head. He tried to swat it, but missed. Trudy tried to freeze it, but nothing happened.

"YOU WERE SUPPOSED TO COME ALONE!" yelled a deep voice from the light as it grew in size and assumed an anthropomorphic shape with a face and arms. In an instant, it grasped hold of Alice, lifting her into the air and dragging her towards a large painting of a mountain.

"Help me!" Alice screamed as she kicked and tried to fight. Barton and Trudy ran to grab her legs but the entity was strong and began sucking her into the painting. Barton had hold of Alice's right leg while Trudy held her left. Alice was disappearing into the painting, only her legs remained. Barton placed his right foot on the wall to secure himself.

"Pull!" he yelled to Trudy, but it was to no avail. The force was too strong and Alice slipped from their grasp leaving them in a crumpled heap on the floor, and Barton holding Alice's right shoe. He touched the painting. Ripples undulated from his touch.

"Shall we go in after her?" Trudy asked. Barton shook his head.

"No, I think we need to get some help," he replied. "This thing is more powerful than any of us."

Chapter Fourteen

Alice was dragged through the painting and dumped onto the floor on the other side of the wall.

"Hold her," the blue entity ordered. Someone close by took hold of Alice's arms and pulled her to her feet. It was so dark, Alice couldn't see who was holding her. "Bring her over here and chain her to the table." Again she was dragged, this time across the room. There were two figures holding her arms, one on each side. The stone floor felt cold beneath her single bare foot. She tripped, but the figures held her firm. Someone lifted her and placed her onto a raised stone platform. She felt her wrists being placed in cold metallic restraints and her ankles in leg irons.

An anonymous voice whispered, "I'm sorry Miss Alice."

"Who are you people? What's happening? Why are you doing this to me?" she screamed. "Let me go – please!"

The entity swirled and floated before her and began to coalesce into a solid form. As her eyes became accustomed to the poor light Alice saw it was, a tall, beautiful woman, dressed in a long white dress that was trimmed with gold.

She and the woman were in a large, dark, seemingly empty chamber, the only exception being five coffin like objects with glass doors, all of which were standing against a wall opposite the platform on which she was chained. She saw that the two dark figures that had restrained her were the skitters – Dorocha and Juan.

"Are you Zephyr?" Alice whispered to the woman. She shivered with terror. A raucous laugh filled the air.

"Do I look like him?" asked the woman.

"I don't know what he looks like," Alice replied.

"Zephyr – my dear, dear Alice – is not here, well he is, but he is not the one you should be worried about," the woman said. "Do you still not recognise me?" Alice shook her head.

"I am Athena you imbecile child!" she announced loudly. She clapped her hands and flame torches on the walls sprang into life.

"Miss Goddessbloom – why? How? What's happening? You're beautiful! And you're not short or old any more. I thought we'd land somewhere that looked like the painting the blue light pulled me through." Alice heard growling. "What's that noise?" she said timidly.

"Dog! Heal" Athena ordered. An enormous, heavy set, black Rottweiler type dog, the size of a large donkey, stepped forward from the darkness and sat obediently next to Athena. When seated, his head was at the same height as Alice's. He snarled at Alice, drooling voraciously and showing his prominent canine teeth. "He's my Hellhound."

"Why hasn't he got a real name?" Alice asked.

"I couldn't be bothered to give him one."

"Where are we? What are you going to do to me?"

"We're in a vault way below the island," Athena continued. "This is where I wiped out the royal families that used to rule this island. In their arrogance they tried to hold dominion over ME! I was a goddess and they tried to subjugate ME! I saved the Ethereals from feudalism by wiping out that lunacy of lycanthropes. Did you know that the collective nouns for werewolves is a lunacy?" Athena ranted. "I fed on them for years – magically, not cannibalistically – I'm not a savage.

No one knows these vaults exist, and I've just had a little magical life top up from your friend Master Tallbrick. He has rejuvenated me, for now. You'll never understand how frustrating it's been for me, over the past hundreds of years, looking after you pathetic little students, with your dribs of magic and your drabs of power. While I had to sit back, growing ever weaker and older. When you were born, Zephyr, my beloved brother, and I formulated a plan to suck the power from your trifecta!"

Alice looked bemused.

"A trifecta! You ignorant girl. Maybe if you listened in class instead of talking back to your elders, you'd know to what I was referring. First your father Sion, second your mother Chloris and thirdly – you! The amount of power we could draw from the three of you could have kept my brother and I young forever. But Zephyr, the fool, fell in love with your mother and backed out at the last moment.

It was I your mother was fighting when she sent you away. I'd already disabled your father but your mother was far more powerful, she was distracted, trying to get you out of my grasp when I struck her down. But now I have you." She grabbed hold of Alice's arm.

"You bitch! I hate you – you bitch! You ruined my life!"

"Watch your language. Do you want to see your parent's deary before you go to sleep with them for ever?" Athena clicked her fingers and lights appeared behind each of the five glass doors. Alice gasped.

"What! I don't believe it! They really are still alive? You've had them here all this time?" Her heart missed a beat. Her mind whirled. Behind the glass doors, three of the coffins were occupied by figures perfectly preserved in golden amber the same way Tallbrick had been. Athena wiped a small patch of dust from the front of one of the doors.

"Here is mummy dearest," she snarled. Alice stretched to try to see the face of the mother she did not remember. Athena moved to the second door.

"This one is your father; he is not looking too well." She moved to the third door. "And this one is my brother Zephyr."

"Mum! Dad! Oh my God! They're really real. They're not dead!" Alice cried, still unable to take in everything that was happening. "Was it you who sent me the note?" she asked Athena.

"Of course. I knew you wouldn't be able to resist the chance to find your parents."

"What are you going to do to me? I don't believe this. All this time you've been pretending to be a nice, sweet old lady, you've been planning to get rid of me? Look, please – I'm really scared – you don't need me. If you count your brother, you've already got three people to suck the life out of."

"Four is better than three," Athena replied. "With all four of your powers I'll be able to rule the universe. A true goddess again. I've kept them alive all this time until I had the full set. You are the final piece. Get out of the way," she ordered the skitters Dorocha and Juan. They backed away into a corner. Athena moved forwards and grasped Alice's shoulders. "I've had enough small talk! Let's get on with this." Her talon like nails dug into Alice's skin. As Athena's grip tightened, Alice felt her life force flowing out of her body. It felt as if there was the weight of a car pushing down on her chest. Her lips tingled and her fingers and feet went numb. Athena's hands and arms began to glow as Alice's life energy travelled up into Athena's arms through golden veins, across her neck and face, until her eyes turned from brown to golden. Alice screamed in agony and her body convulsed. The pain was unbearable.

"Stop! Please stop! It really hurts. You're killing me!" she begged.

Athena ignored Alice's cries.

"Please forgive me madam," Dorocha said timidly. "But might it not be advisable to let Miss Alice rest for a while. She needs to be strong enough to survive the preservation process." Athena glared at him.

"Shut up!" she hissed as she continued her attack. "I've never experienced power like this. It's intoxicating." Alice's body reeled in pain and she screamed again.

"But it looks as if she's dying madam," Juan whispered. Athena paused for an instant and thought. She removed her hands from Alice's shoulders.

Alice gasped for air. Even though the attack had stopped the agony continued spreading through every nerve of her body from her ears to her toes.

"Oh my God! How can anything be this painful!" A random thought flashed through Alice's mind - *I'm going to die with only one shoe on. I will not die. I will not die. I will not die.* Relieved that Athena had stopped her assault for the moment, Alice closed her eyes and pretended to be unconscious but tears ran from the corners of her eyes and down her cheeks.

"Get her ready!" Athena ordered. Dorocha stepped forward and took a glowing amber stick from his pocket. He approached Alice and began waving the stick over her seemingly unconscious body. The pain in her extremities began to abate but she started to feel sticky.

"Not so fast!" said a man's voice from behind Athena. "Athena we were supposed to do this together." Alice opened her eyes and gasped as she turned her head to see Herb.

"You're in this with her? Herb please help me," Alice whimpered, desperately wanting his help and unable to comprehend his betrayal. Athena turned to face him.

"Dog! Watch her!" Athena ordered. The dog

obediently sat to the side of the platform Alice was chained to. Alice looked into his red eyes and sensed sadness, but he growled at her. "How did you find this place?" Athena asked Herb angrily.

"I placed a tracking device in Alice's mobile phone. I know she never goes anywhere without the damn thing and I teleported here." Herb winked at Alice.

"Whatever! Why should I share my power with anyone? I am a GODDESS!" Athena exclaimed. Her eyes turned from golden to red and beams shot from them casting Herb backwards. She flicked her wrist, pinning him against the wall. "What the Hell! I have a spare chamber – maybe I'll take your powers as well," she laughed. She threw open the door to one of the unoccupied chambers, but instantly changed her mind. "But then maybe I'll just kill you."

"Alice doesn't even have her full powers yet. Why didn't you wait till her birthday?" Herb gasped, trying to distract Athena.

"I got bored – like I am now!" An invisible force tightened around Herb's neck.

"Alice – if you're going to do something – now would be a good time!" he pleaded

"Me!" she squealed. Athena shot her an evil glance. "I'm chained to a bloody table. I'm too weak. She's took all my energy! I can't do anything. I don't know what to do, and that dog might get me!"

"Now Alice!" he yelled. She closed her eyes to concentrate. "Or we're both dead."

"Break, damn you," she told the shackles that bound her. Nothing happened. "It's no good Herb. I'm not strong enough."

"Alice – please!" he begged with his last breath as he clutched at the invisible force around his neck.

"Please don't hurt me," she whispered to Dog.

"Don't even think about it!" Athena hissed at Alice,

ever tightening her grip around Herb's throat. "I'll deal with you in a minute."

"Don't! You're killing him," Alice screamed. Dog glared at her. Herb's face was turning purple as Athena squeezed his windpipe with her unseen might.

A memory flashed through her mind – the fire in the school cupboard and the car on the Briggs' driveway setting alight. She'd done that without any effort. Alice closed her eyes once more and concentrated. She bit her top lip and screwed up her eyes. In that instant Athena's hair spontaneously burst into flames.

"Aaargh!" Athena screamed as she realised what was happening. She released her hold on Herb's throat slightly as she batted the flames on her head with her hands until they were out.

Alice concentrated again with all her might.

"Break, damn you - BREAK!" This time the ankle and wrist bracelets snapped open and she rolled off the platform to the right, the opposite side from where Dog sat, and onto the floor. From a standing bound Dog leapt over the table. Alice snapped her fingers and Dog froze mid air. It was the first time she'd ever frozen anything and she proudly rose to her feet.

Athena, however, was not frozen. With another flick of her wrist Athena threw Alice backwards. Alice's head hit the wall, momentarily dazing her. It was enough to unfreeze dog who landed, then stood over Alice barking and snarling in her face.

"No! I've had enough of this," Alice said adamantly. She raised her right hand and stared at Dog. "Back off or I'll set your head on fire too!" she warned him. Dog stood his ground but thoughtfully stayed where he was. As Athena concentrated on Herb, Alice crawled across the floor. Alice placed her left hand on the glass door of her mother's compartment. She instantly felt power flowing through her, reviving her, and once more rose to her feet. Alice imagined that draining energy from her mother could injure Chloris further, but Alice knew she had to be stronger if she was going to beat Athena. However, she knew the power boost wasn't enough. She remembered the Impundulu egg she wore around her neck and snatched it breaking the chain. She grasped it tightly in her right fist. The power surged through her. "Let him go!" Alice yelled. Athena turned to Alice, releasing her hold on Herb. He fell to the floor.

"You think you can take me – you arrogant pipsqueak," Athena said directing the red eye light rays at Alice. Alice stood firm and did not move.

"You're not a goddess!" Alice said as she embraced the new power she commanded, even her voice sounded deeper. "You've never created anything!" With new found strength, she drew on the Impundulu egg and raised a blue energy force field before her. As Athena's eye beams hit the shield it sparked and exploded but Alice stood firm. Athena intensified her attack but the shield held. Athena's hair reignited but she ignored the flames. Dog ran away, yelping in fear. Dorocha and Juan followed him. With a twist of the force field Alice deflected the beams back to Athena's eyes. Athena finally screamed with rage and pain and fell to her knees.

"No!" she sneered through gritted teeth. "You cannot beat me. You're just a child!"

"Yeah! I'm the kid who's just kicked your ass!" Alice snarled. With a hiss, the room filled with sparks, and the beams burned out Athena's eyes leaving blackened, smoking holes in her skull.

"Take that, you evil bitch!" Alice exclaimed. "And only my cousin is allowed to call me pipsqueak!"

At that moment Sala'huddin, Trudy, Barton, Eloise, Plasadera, and all the djinn students fell through the wall.

"We've come to rescue you!" Barton announced. Alice ran to her cousin and hugged him.

"What happened here? Why is he here?" Sala'huddin asked pointing to Herb.

"This is my mum and dad," she said pointing to the glass chambers. "THEY'RE ALIVE! It was Athena – Miss Goddessbloom, not Zephyr, who was after me. She's been keeping them alive down here and feeding off their magic and she was going to put me in one of these cases and feed off me too. And she nearly killed me! And it really hurt! Then Herb came and distracted her and I froze the dog, then she turned her laser beams on me and 'POW' there were sparks and explosions everywhere and I zapped her eyes out. It was scary but I was really cool." She kissed her Impundulu egg and put it in her pocket. Dog, Dorocha and Juan submissively crawled out of the shadows, all whimpering.

"I brought your shoe," Barton said and gave Alice her errant footwear. Alice took it from him and smiled as she slipped it on to her foot.

"Thanks mate," she said.

"You did this to Alice didn't you Herb? You were working with Athena all along, weren't you Herb?" Sala'huddin shouted accusingly. Herb shook his head.

"No. Ask your mother," he gasped. Released from Athena's strangle hold he could now breathe and talk. "I knew Athena was up to something but I thought she was working with Zephyr so Rosebay and I pretended to be plotting with her. I didn't know these particular underground chambers existed and had no idea she was keeping Chloris and Sion here. For all these years I too thought they were dead."

"What do you mean – ask my mother?" Sala'huddin butted in.

"When we met on Zelda I told her my plan to find

out what Athena was up to. That's why she let me bring Alice back here."

"So Alice was bait and my mum went along with it? I don't believe it. You're lying."

"I'm sorry Alice. Before I came to Zelda, Tallbrick confided that he believed Sion and Chloris may still be alive. I didn't really believe him but I told your mother and we together we decided that this was the only way to find out if it was true and find your parents," Herb replied as he picked himself up from the floor and knocked the dust from his clothes. "I have been tracking you, and Noorjahan trusted me to take care of you."

Athena was rolling on the ground, clutching her eye sockets, and moaning in pain. Her hair was still smouldering.

"No, no, no," she sobbed. Alice felt like kicking her while she was down, but thought better of it.

"Can we just get my mum and dad out of these things?" Alice asked.

**

"So tell me – how did you get back to the school to raise the alarm?" Alice asked Trudy and Barton the next morning over breakfast.

"We went back and thawed out Townie just enough so she could talk and she showed us how to open the staircase by moving a sequence of books on the shelves. Using the capital letter of each author's name of four books – Osprey – Penfold – Euchlid – Nefarious - to spell the word OPEN. We left Townie there cos her legs were weak from being frozen for weeks," said Barton. "We thought the djinn were more trustworthy than the warlocks...."

"Less scary, more like," Trudy put in.

137

"So we went and told your cousin what had happened and he got everyone else and we all went back down the secret staircase, and then we all jumped through the painting," Barton gabbled without taking a breath and with a milk moustache under his nose. "It was really cool when there was a gang of us doing it."

"Are your mum and dad going to be alright?" Trudy asked.

"The infirmary looks like a war zone. Mum and dad have been taken out of those chamber thingies and are still unconscious and a witches' coven are doing spells and things to make them better, but they've got drips and real medicine as well. I've been sitting with them most of the night, but I got hungry. Tallbrick is being de-amberfied and Townie is being treated for hypothermia and Nurse Carbunkle says she has got to do physiotherapy cos her muscles got atrophied. Apparently it was Miss Goddessbloom who drugged my drink with wingot root at the All Hallows Eve party and told Townie to only give it to me. Townie hadn't got any idea what was in it. Herb's got a sore throat from where Athena tried to strangle him."

"Good! What about Athena and Zephyr?" Barton asked.

"Zephyr is being left in his stasis chamber and Athena is being put in one as we speak. They bandaged up her head and her eyes but she'll never see again. And she's bald."

"Serves them right," Barton said. "Who's going to run the school now and who's going to look after that huge dog?"

"I think either Herb or Rosebay Thistledown will run the school," Trudy replied.

"And Herb's taking the dog," Alice said.

"Your cousin reckons Herb was in on it," Barton said.

"I know! But for now we have to trust him," Alice replied. "Herb has had plenty of opportunity to hurt me, if he'd wanted to. Plus my aunty trusted him."

"What about the skitters Dorocha and Juan? They helped Miss Goddessbloom to hurt you."

"Herb says they were just following orders – like soldiers on the losing side of a battle. So they've been put to work cleaning out the sewers – FOR EVER! Ha, ha!" Alice laughed.

"Hey with all this happening I almost forgot – tonight's the Winter Solstice. Good ole St Nick is due for his annual appearance," said Barton cheerfully.

**

That evening the whole school assembled in the dining room after supper. The hall was decorated with holly and mistletoe and a thousand candles illuminated the room. The roof opened and all the children looked skywards into the night as they heard the sleigh bells on St Nicolas' sled. He circled the school and landed on the front lawn.

The students formed a procession and as they exited the dining hall, a skitter gave each child a green cloak to keep them warm, and they were each handed a candle. The skitters formed a line behind the children. The large front doors were fully opened and the children filed out in pairs onto the lawn. The Mer people from Lightwold had brought their children to the school to meet St Nicholas and were outside waiting for the students to join them.

St Nicolas' sleigh pulled by six reindeers with glistening antlers, had settled in the centre of the lawn. Uhh, Ba, Guh, Ba and Ba all wore garlands made of evergreen boughs, mistletoe and holly. St Nicolas stood on his sleigh and the children approached him in turn.

He greeted each student and skitter and Mer child warmly, and handed them an individual gift.

Unlike the fat, jolly Santa dressed in red, of the human world, St Nicolas was a tall, elegant man who wore a long green cloak, trimmed in ermine. He had a long, silky white beard. Alice followed Trudy, and as her turn approached her stomach did somersaults with excitement. It looked to her as if St Nicholas was glowing.

I can't believe he's real, she thought.

"Alice Devises," he said with a huge smile as she stepped forward. "You've had a tumultuous few months Alice." She nodded. "Now what can I possibly give you?" he said reaching into his sack.

"Sir," she replied. "Unless you can make my mum and dad get better, I already have everything I've ever wanted. I have found my family."

St Nicholas smiled kindly.

"If I could heal your parents I would my child, but unfortunately that is beyond even my power," he said sadly.

"I understand," Alice replied.

"How would you like a hand held, electronic games console?" St Nicholas asked.

"Yeah! That would be good too!" she replied cheekily. They laughed together and Alice graciously accepted the gift.

Alice joined Trudy and Barton and hugged them. She waved to Sala'huddin who was surrounded by his usual entourage. Gentle flakes of snow began to fall. The entire school – children, faculty, Mer people and skitters – encircled St Nicholas and the reindeers and lit their candles. An elfin choir sang a haunting melody.

"This is truly the most awesome day of my life so far!" Alice cried as she stood arm in arm with Trudy and Barton. "I can't wait for what happens next!"

The End

.

www.ingramcontent.com/pod-product-compliance
Lightning Source LLC
Chambersburg PA
CBHW030130260626
47156CB00008B/2883